'I just have to *say* it, don't I? Steve, I'm pregnant.'

Whump!

That was the sound of his backside hitting the couch with force. He suddenly knew what the expression 'legs turning to jelly' meant, in a way he never had before. Beyond the beating of blood in his head, he had wit enough to understand at once that his first reaction to this news was critical. Still, the only thing he could come up with at first was, 'That's a surprise.'

'I know.' She nodded. She flushed, then smiled, and that gave him his first clue.

She's thrilled.

After living in the USA for nearly eight years, **Lilian Darcy** is back in her native Australia with her American historian husband and their four young children. More than ever, writing is a treat for her now, looked forward to and luxuriated in like a hot bath after a hard day. She likes to create modern heroes and heroines with good doses of zest and humour in their make-up, and relishes the opportunity that the medical series gives her for dealing with genuine, gripping drama in romance and in daily life. She finds research fascinating too—everything from attacking learned medical tomes to spending a day in a maternity ward.

Recent titles by the same author:

THE SURGEON'S LOVE-CHILD

BY
LILIAN DARCY

First published in Great Britain 2002
Large Print edition 2002
Harlequin Mills & Boon Limited,
Eton House, 18-24 Paradise Road,
Richmond, Surrey TW9 1SR

© Lilian Darcy 2002

ISBN 0 263 17310 0

Set in Times Roman 16½ on 17 pt.
17-0902-50879

Printed and bound in Great Britain
by Antony Rowe Ltd, Chippenham, Wiltshire

CHAPTER ONE

HE WAS holding up a sign with her name on it, but he wasn't Terry Davis.

Definitely not.

Terry wouldn't have needed a sign. He and Candace had known each other, on and off, for years. She would have recognised his weatherbeaten face at once, and he would have seen her coming towards him through the milling crowd of arrivals at Sydney's international airport. He would have smiled.

This man wasn't smiling. He hadn't seen her yet. He hadn't realised that Candace had spotted her name, scrawled quickly by hand in black felt-tip pen on a makeshift rectangle of cardboard, and that she was zeroing in on it.

This man looked much younger than Terry. Early thirties, tall and fit and medium dark, with a body that somehow managed to be both solid and lean at the same time. He was wearing jeans and a navy T-shirt that hugged his form closely. In contrast, Terry was well past fifty, and had always looked his age. He never wore jeans.

Candace herself—DR CANDACE FLETCHER, as the sign correctly stated—was thirty-eight years old and intensely conscious of the fact. She had been for months and was, suddenly, particularly conscious of it now. It had been twenty-four hours since she had left Boston. She must look like a dog's breakfast, despite a recent freshening in the unappealing cubicle of the aircraft toilet.

She reached the stranger and his sign, and was tempted to wave a hand in front of his face. Hell-o-o-o! I'm here! He was still scanning the crowd with a frown etched across his high, squarish forehead. Apparently, she didn't look like her name.

'Are you waiting for me?'

The frown cleared at once. 'With insufficient vigilance, obviously, Dr Fletcher. You sneaked up on me.'

'I did think about waving.'

'Probably not what you expected. I should have been Terry.'

'Mmm.'

She almost blurted out that not much in her life had gone according to expectations over the past year and more, but managed to keep the words back. Dear God, it would be so easy to get emotional!

'I'll explain as we head to the car,' he said.

'Sounds good.'

Unobtrusively, he took control of the luggage cart and began to wheel it towards the exit. She walked beside him, matching his pace.

'I'm Steve, by the way. Steve Colton. You'll be seeing me in Theatre fairly regularly. I'm often rostered to handle the anaesthesia. Terry's wife is…not well. That's why he couldn't make it.'

'Oh, no!' Candace said. 'That's too bad! It isn't serious, I hope.'

'So do I,' he answered soberly. 'But I'm actually her GP, so I can't really talk about it. Is this all of your luggage?'

'This is it,' she confirmed. Three suitcases and a box, for a one-year stay. 'My mother helped me pack, and she's very strict.'

'Travels light?'

'Arrives light. Leaves heavy. She's convinced that Australia will have glorious shopping possibilities, thanks to the state of your dollar.'

'She's right, if you can find anything you want to buy. Terry told you Narralee's not a big place, I hope. Not exactly a shopper's heaven.'

'Yes, but my mother has a bloodhound's nose for good places to spend money. And Terry also told me Sydney makes a great weekend getaway, only a three-and-a-half-hour drive. Oh! Which means you're making a seven-hour round trip to pick me up,' she realised aloud, 'and I haven't thanked you yet.'

'Plenty of time for that.'

'Three and a half hours, in fact.'

They both laughed.

He seemed nice, Candace decided. The kind of well-mannered yet easygoing Australian male she'd heard good things about and seen—in somewhat exaggerated form—in various movies over the years. Three and a half hours, plus a stop for a snack, maybe. This shouldn't be any kind of a penance...

And it wasn't. Far from it.

They talked for a while, about the obvious things. Her journey. The city of Sydney. She commented on its red-tiled roofs, bright in the March morning sunlight, and all the aqua blue ovals and rectangles of the swimming pools she'd seen from above in the sprawl of suburban back yards as the plane had come in to land.

Then they left human habitation behind and crossed the wild, wind-scoured terrain of a national park. Steve Colton stopped asking questions and giving out helpful tourist information. Candace pretended to sleep.

She had been doing a lot of that lately—lying in bed with her brain buzzing and the shrill whistle of tinnitus in her ears, totally exhausted, miles from sleep and not fooling herself for a second.

Todd was sleeping with Brittany for six months and I never knew.

He said our marriage was empty long before that. Was he right? If there hadn't been that electrical problem at the hospital that day, and they hadn't cancelled elective surgery... If I hadn't actually walked in on them, naked together in our marital bed... How long before I'd have found out? How long before he would have drummed up the courage to leave? Coming home to find them in bed was bad enough, but having them announce Brittany's pregnancy before our divorce was even finalised was even worse.

I guess in a way I'm glad Maddy decided not to come to Australia with me—although that hurts, too, to think she's so positive that she'll be fine without her mother—because at least, out there, I'll be able to be alone. I won't have to pretend.

And here she was, pretending already.

Much easier to pretend to a newly met male colleague than to an emotional fifteen-year-old daughter, however. By hook or by crook, Candace *wasn't* going to ruin Maddy's relationship with her father. She had no right to do that—to deprive her daughter of something very precious and necessary in Maddy's life purely in order to enact revenge on Todd, when maybe…probably…the blame wasn't all on his side. She had to behave rationally, not let Maddy see quite how deeply ran her sense of betrayal.

But, oh, that huge, glowing and healthily advanced pregnancy of Brittany's *hurt*! She was due in just a few weeks…

The car slowed. It stopped. Then there was silence. She opened her eyes. Dr Colton was watching her. No, *Steve*. She couldn't possibly call him Dr Colton! He had to be a good five or six years younger than she was, and she had been told that Australians were informal people.

'Are we here?' she asked vaguely. She had no idea how long her mind had been churning while her eyes had flickered behind their closed lids.

'No,' he said, 'But I thought it was probably hours since they gave you breakfast on the plane. It was a toss-up between letting you sleep and getting you fed. Did I pick the right one?'

'I wasn't asleep,' she admitted, finding it easier to be honest with him than she had expected. 'Just thinking.'

'That can give you an appetite.'

She smiled. 'It has. Or something has.'

'Rightio, then.'

Rightio? Weird word! Cute, actually. The difference, the newness of it in his easy accent, blew across the raw-burned surface of her soul like a gentle puff of wind, and she was still smiling as she got out of the car.

He hadn't gone so far as to open the door for her. She might have mistrusted that degree of chivalry. But he was standing there waiting, and he reached out a hand to steady her as she stood up.

The kerb was unexpectedly high. She held onto him, closing her fingers around a forearm that was bare and warm and ropy with muscle, while his hand remained cupped beneath her elbow.

'Oh-h! The sidewalk is going up and down,' she said.

'Having your own personal earthquake?'

'No, it's more gentle than that. A kind of quavery undulation.'

He laughed. 'It's that long flight, and the beginnings of jet-lag. What time is it now in Boston?'

'Um...'

'Let's see...'

They both began a mental calculation.

'Sydney is sixteen hours ahead,' she supplied. 'Which means...'

He got there first. 'Yesterday evening, then. Around sevenish. You probably *are* hungry in that case, and an empty stomach wouldn't be helping.'

'No,' she agreed, although this wobbly sidewalk was probably more the result of months of stress and inadequate sleep than a mere sixteen-hour time difference and a few hours without food.

'Shall I let go?' he asked cheerfully.

'Not yet.'

It seemed like a long time since she'd had a man's physical support, and it felt better than she could have imagined. He wasn't in a hurry. He didn't have an agenda. He was polite and steady, and she felt very safe.

'OK,' he said, tightening his grip a little.

Their eyes met and held for a moment before they both looked away. He was very good-looking. She hadn't taken in this fact until now. It was in the shape of his face—the square forehead, the strong cheekbones and chin. It was in his easy, even smile, too, and in what that smile did to his blue eyes. They twinkled and softened, and looked a little wicked.

But this wasn't just about looks, she realised. This was about—

Dear heaven, we're going to have an affair!

The thought sliced into her mind without a shadow of warning, leaving her breathless. She could almost see it—the alluring progression of it—laid out before her like the squares on a life-sized Monopoly board, improbably perfect. A sizzlingly hot, totally heedless, carefree, life-affirming, fabulous affair, which would come to a painless, mutually-agreed-upon end some time before she was due to head home to that much chillier place called Real Life.

She dropped his delicious, masculine forearm like a live snake, her heart pounding.

This doesn't happen to me. The whole idea is ridiculous. I don't have intuitions like this. I'm scared. Would I really want something like that? No! Surely I wouldn't! And surely I'm wrong! Of course I'm wrong!

'I'm starving,' she said aloud.

Wow.

Say it again.

Wow.

Don't let it show on your face, Steve.

This woman is... No, she's not gorgeous. Not even pretty. Something much better, and much more interesting. She's magnetic, womanly, responsive.

He hadn't felt it at first. He had been too busy thinking about the last time he'd been at Sydney airport, several months ago, seeing Agnetha off on her flight back home to Sweden.

The memory was like a splinter in his thumb. Yes, sure, he knew it wasn't a major wound, but that didn't stop it from hurting. And it had preoccupied him more than he'd wanted it to, during his wait for the visiting American doctor.

Did I even *consider* getting serious, asking Agnetha to marry me? No!

If she'd asked me to go to Sweden with her, would I have gone? No!

So what's my problem?

One of sheer, bloody male ego, perhaps. He was...*miffed*...that Agnetha had apparently viewed him the same way she'd viewed the second-hand surfboard she'd bought at the surf shop in Narralee. Something to be enjoyed during her stay, but not something to take home with her, except in a photo or two. The surfboard was still in the back shed, beside his own. Agnetha had smiled as she'd waved goodbye. Five months down the track, she hadn't even sent a postcard.

Now, here was another visitor from the northern hemisphere, equipped with what was known as special needs registration so that she could work here in a rural hospital in her surgical specialty. She was about fifteen years older than Agnetha. She had a long, thick, satisfying rope of honey-gold hair, bound back in a braid, instead of a fine thatch of short, Scandinavian blonde.

She had skin that would probably freckle like bits of melted milk chocolate under the Australian sun, while Agnetha's skin had remained a perfect pale gold. Candace had almond-shaped eyes like brown pebbles, polished by the sea, while Agnetha's were blue and clear and round. She had a ripe, luscious figure, with exquisitely full breasts and rounded hips, instead of a lean, almost boyish slimness.

And she had a lot more *living* evident in her face.

Terry had told him that Dr Fletcher had been divorced last year, and that she had a fifteen-year-old daughter. Well, it showed. Some of the sadness and complexity showed, around her tawny eyes and her generous mouth. For some reason, it actually added to the quiet richness of her unconventional beauty.

There was one thing that Candace Fletcher and Agnetha Thorhus had in common, however. With both of them, Steve had recognised within an hour or two of meeting them that there was a definite, undeniable and very bewitching spark. In this case, he wasn't yet sure what he intended to do about it.

He took Candace to the café that was housed in the little town's former bank. The place had a lot of charm, and excellent Devonshire teas.

'My stomach is suddenly saying dinner, very loudly, at eleven-thirty in the morning,' Candace confessed, so she began with a bowl of pumpkin soup, some salad and a hot, buttered roll. Then she moved on to scones with strawberry jam and whipped cream.

Not particularly hungry himself, Steve drank black coffee while he sat back and watched her eat. She was good at it. Just the right combination of fastidiousness and relish. Her response to the whipped cream was particularly appealing, and when she had finished there was a tiny beauty spot of white froth left just beyond the corner of her mouth.

Knowing that it wasn't just a casual gesture, he leaned forward and used the tip of one finger to wipe it off. She didn't object. Didn't even look startled.

She knows, he thought, and felt an odd little flutter inside his chest which he didn't have a name for.

She knows, too, just the way I do. She knows that something could happen between us. Whether it will or not, neither of us has decided yet...

It was a very pretty drive, Candace decided.

Dairy country, according to Steve. To the right, cliff-like escarpments rose above thick forests of eucalypts, but as the steepness of the terrain shelved away, the forest gave way to fenced farmland that was lush and green. To the left, in the distance, Candace glimpsed the sea. It twinkled in the sun like Steve Colton's eyes.

And I'll be looking at this sight every single day for the next year...

Looking at the sea, not the eyes.

Terry had arranged the rental of a furnished beach cottage for her, sending details, including photographs, of three or four for her to choose from. Narralee wasn't quite on the coast but a mile or two inland, built on the banks of a river's coastal estuary.

She hadn't wanted the tameness and tranquillity of a river, no matter how pretty it was. She'd wanted the sea, fresh and wild and as solitary as possible, and the place she'd selected was in a little seaside community called Taylor's Beach, about ten minutes' drive away.

Steve had the address, and the keys. As soon as he pulled into the short driveway, she knew that the house and its setting were going to go way beyond her expectations. The house was built high, with the utilitarian parts beneath— carport, laundry, storage. On top, with magnificent views of the sea, were the living areas. There were other houses close by but, with tangles of bushland garden surrounding them, they didn't impinge.

Steve helped Candace carry her luggage inside, then watched with a grin on his face as she simply wandered from room to room, uttering incoherent exclamations of pleasure.

'You like it, then?' he asked finally, when she returned to stand, woolly-witted, in front of the French windows that opened onto a shaded deck.

'It's perfect!'

'I told Terry you'd pick this one if you were any good at reading photographs.'

'They didn't do it justice.'

'How about my descriptions?'

'Oh, it was you who wrote those?'

'I tried to be objective, but probably didn't succeed. I'm incurably biased. Couldn't imagine why anyone *wouldn't* want to live along this stretch of beach.'

'So where do you live?'

'Five doors down.'

'Right.' She nodded, and looked quickly out at the ocean again before their eyes could meet. Five doors down. That had the potential to be very convenient. 'Um, I like the interior, too, as well as the setting and the views,' she added, speaking too fast.

The house wasn't elaborate or huge. There was an open-plan lounge and dining room, a modern kitchen, a generous bathroom and two airy bedrooms, one furnished with twin beds, one with a queen-size. But with a whole world of sand and ocean and sky out there, she didn't need interior space. The rooms were decorated in summery blues and yellows, with light, casual touches of good taste in the occasional piece of ceramic work or glassware.

Steve opened the French windows, and a sea breeze combed through the outer screens and puffed air into the full-length blue and yellow curtains, which were pulled back on their tracks to reveal the view. Candace went out onto the deck, willing him not to follow her. She could smell the fresh salt in the air at once.

Here on the deck, the outdoor furniture was made of cane. It didn't normally appeal to her, but fitted in this setting. Yes, she would eat here at this little cane and glass table and watch the ocean, every chance she got...

'I think Linda was planning to pick up some basic supplies for you,' Steve said behind her, just inside. 'Shall I check the fridge?'

'Thanks.'

'Then I ought to head off. I have appointments at my practice, starting at two.'

'You've been terrific.' She stepped back into the cool living room.

They were both being very neutral and polite with each other now.

'Terry wants me to bring you into the hospital tomorrow morning, to meet everyone and get you orientated a little before you start in earnest on Monday. We've had to send a lot of our general surgery patients further north since before Christmas, when Dr Elphick retired. Quite a few people chose to postpone their operations, though, so you'll be busy straight away.'

'Yes, I was going to ask about all that. And about the other two hospitals I'm covering as well.'

'Better talk to Terry. Is it all right if I pick you up at eight-thirty?'

'I'll be ready.'

She watched as he opened the fridge and the pantry. He confirmed, 'Yes, Linda's been here.'

'Should I know about Linda?'

'Linda Gardner, our local ob. You're sharing professional rooms with her. Terry arranged it. With luck you'll meet her tomorrow. Looks like she's decided you'll have eggs for dinner. Unless you phone out for take-away.'

'The phone's connected, then?' She was pleased to hear it.

'Yep. Of course, you'll want to ring home, won't you?'

Another odd word. Ring, instead of call. Quaint. Cute.

'Um, where is it, I wonder? I can't see it.'

'Think I noticed it by the bed.'

'Thanks. I won't keep you.'

'See you tomorrow, then.'

Seconds later, he was loping down the steps at the side of the house to his car.

Alone. Candace was alone, the way she had craved to be for months. Finding a plastic pitcher of iced water in the fridge, she poured herself a glass. Saw the eggs Steve had mentioned and decided that, yes, they'd be fine for her evening meal. If she lasted that long. The floor of the house was rocking up and down like the deck of a boat. Glass in hand, she went back through the French doors and onto the deck to watch the sea.

Just me, with the ocean for company.

It felt different to what she had expected. It was a happier, zestier feeling. She had more than half expected to zero right in on that comfortable-looking bed, covered in an intricately pieced patchwork quilt, and sob her eyes out.

In fact, she'd actually *planned* to indulge in the painfully luxurious release of being able to cry for hours, as stormily as she wanted to, without the possibility of interruption.

But, no, she didn't want to cry now after all.

Mom was the one who had suggested this whole thing. Mom, the redoubtable, loving Elaine West.

'Couldn't you go away, darling?' she had said five months ago, when Candace had gone to her with the blind pain of a wounded animal, freshly ripped apart by the news of Brittany's pregnancy.

'I don't know if I can stand it, Mom,' she had gasped, barely able to speak. 'She's radiant, while he's...oh...already shopping for cigars. Not literally, but—'

'I know what you mean, Candy.'

'They had prenatal testing and they already know it's a boy. Suddenly it turns out that Todd has "always wanted a son". To me, he spent years arguing that one child was enough. Expensive enough. Sacrifice enough. Career-threatening enough. For his sake, I gave away the bassinet and the baby clothes. I told myself he was right. That Maddy was enough. But, oh, I wanted another baby! And now—'

'Couldn't you go away?' Elaine said.

'Away?'

'Some kind of professional fellowship or exchange. Or a temporary position. In Alaska, or somewhere.'

'*Alaska?*'

'You don't need them on your doorstep, Candy.' Her mother was the only person in the world who was ever permitted to call her Candy, and even then only at times, when she needed to feel six years old again, nourishing her soul with a mother's wisdom. 'You don't need to run into Brittany at the gym—'

'Ha! As if I still go to the gym!'

Eighteen months ago, Todd had taken out a family membership, saying they both needed to get fitter. Brittany, aged twenty-five to Todd's forty-four, taught aerobics there. Todd had quickly become very fit indeed. End of story. Candace felt personally insulted that the whole thing was such a cliché.

'Or at the hospital.'

'The *hospital*?'

'Prenatal check-ups. Your OB/GYN has her practice in the hospital's adjoining professional building, doesn't she?'

'Of course, you're right. I know I'll see her. Todd and I have a daughter together, remember? Occasionally we actually pass her back and forth at his place, instead of on safe, neutral terrain like school or the mall. Occasionally we even speak to each other.' The words were hard with bitterness.

'Maybe Maddy would like to get away, too?' Elaine had suggested.

But when Candace had remembered Terry Davis's comment, at a recent international medical conference, that rural Australia was chronically short of medical specialists, and had teed up this temporary appointment, Maddy had elected to stay behind with her father.

It hadn't been in any sense a rejection of Candace. She knew that. It was about friends and routine, not about choosing one parent over the other, but it still hurt all the same.

She's growing up. I'll miss her more than she misses me. But Mom was right. This was probably the best thing I could have done.

After finishing her iced water, she found the phone by the bed. Called Maddy first. Heard Brittany's perky voice, which quickly crystallised into glassy, high-pitched politeness when she realised who was on the other end of the line.

Candace had a brief conversation with Maddy, then called her mother, who said 'See!' in a very satisfied voice when she heard about the beachfront cottage and the acres of sea and sky. 'Have you explored?'

'I haven't even unpacked!'

'Dr Davis met you on time?'

'Uh, no, he had to delegate to a colleague, but it worked out fine.'

And I managed to avoid mentioning Steve's name, which I'm relieved about, and I know exactly why I didn't want to mention it, which is unsettling me like anything...

When Candace had put down the phone, she looked at the suitcases and the box, stuck her tongue out at them and said in her best new millennium teen-speak, 'You think I'm gonna unpack you right now, when there's that beach out there? Like, as if!'

She walked the length of the beach twice, breathing the air and letting the cool water froth around her ankles. Then she unpacked, showered, made and ate scrambled eggs on toast, and conked out at seven in the evening in the big, comfortable bed with the sound of the sea in her ears.

She fell asleep as suddenly as if someone had opened up a panel in her back and removed the batteries.

CHAPTER TWO

IT WAS the best night's sleep Candace had had in months, and it lasted until almost five the next morning. This meant she had plenty of time to iron a skirt and blouse, have another shower and eat breakfast on the deck, watching the sun rise over the sea. She was ready for Steve Colton at eight-thirty.

He was prompt, and if she'd had any sort of a theory overnight that yesterday's intuitive sense of chemistry had been only a product of her jet-lagged disorientation, that theory was knocked on the head at once.

The chemistry was still there, invisible, intangible, lighter than air, yet as real as a third person with them in the room. Neither of them acknowledged it in any way. They didn't get close enough to touch. Any eye contact they chanced to make was snapped apart again in milliseconds.

But, oh, it was there, and she was convinced he felt it, too.

She spent half an hour with Terry at the Narralee District Hospital. He had earned a certain seniority, having been a visiting medical officer in general surgery here for over twenty-five years, but in fact there wasn't the official hierarchy of medical staff that Candace was used to.

There wasn't very much that she was used to at all! It was quite a contrast to come from a 600-bed high-rise American city hospital to this low, rambling, red-brick building, which housed a mere fifty beds.

'And six of those are political,' Terry said darkly.

'Political?'

'They're not beds at all, in most people's definition. We have six reclining chairs where day-surgery patients recover until we're satisfied that fluids are going in one end and coming out the other. But those six chairs make the numbers look better, so beds they've become and beds they'll remain.'

He sounded tired and tense, and Candace longed to urge him, Go. Someone else can show me around.

Steve Colton, maybe? He'd muttered something about 'errands' after he'd deposited her into Terry's care, and then he had disappeared. She was disturbed to realise that she was wondering, in the back of her mind, when she'd see him again.

She wanted to tell Terry, The tour can wait. I know you're anxious to be on your way.

Terry was taking his wife, Myrna, up to Sydney today for a consultation with a top oncologist. The result of her second mammogram and fine-needle aspiration had come back yesterday afternoon, and there was no longer any doubt about the diagnosis. It was breast cancer.

They could only hope that it had been caught early, and Terry was clearly racked with worry. He was also behaving stubbornly in his insistence on a tour and a talk. He must feel as if he had let Candace down by not meeting her at the airport yesterday, and was determined to make up for it.

Accepting that she would only delay his departure if she kept apologising for her bad timing, Candace tried to ask a few intelligent questions and keep the pace brisk.

'No full-time doctors here at all?'

'No, we manage purely with Visiting Medical Officers. The local GPs cover the emergency department and the on-call roster, assist with surgery and handle anaesthesia. Steve probably mentioned that.'

'Yes, he did, but not in any detail.'

'Then there are about half a dozen of us who handle various specialities, travelling between several small hospitals in the region, as you'll be doing. You can work out your own time-table, within certain constraints. Linda Gardner has space in her rooms, and will share her staff with you.'

'Yes, Steve told me. Thanks for arranging it. I'm looking forward to meeting her.'

'You'll like her, I think. She's married with two teenagers.'

'We'll have something in common in that area, then!'

'Basically, you'll probably want to operate one day a week here in Narralee, and a day every fortnight at Harpoon Bay and Shoalwater.'

'A slower pace than I'm used to.'

'Enjoy it!'

'Oh, I intend to.'

The hospital had already created a pleasing impression. Its red-tiled roof had pale green lichen growing on it, attesting to its comfortable age. Above what must once have been the main entrance, the date '1936' was carved. Mature eucalyptus trees shaded thick couch-grass lawns, and windows tinted with a gold reflective film ran all along one side of the building.

Most of the windows were open, providing a volume of fresh, mild air that was unheard of in Candace's experience. In Boston, winters were arctic, summers were steamy and hospitals had air-conditioning.

With its pink walls and mottled linoleum floors, the place was too clean and cheerful to be called shabby, and there was an atmosphere of peace, underlaid by a low buzz of unhurried activity which suggested that hospitals didn't have to be nearly as dramatic and hectic as they always seemed on prime-time television.

Terry doggedly tramped the building from one end to the other on their tour. He showed Candace the eight-bed maternity unit, which opened onto a shaded veranda. He took her through the four-bed high-dependency unit, the aged-care rehab beds, day surgery, the pharmacy, Emergency and Physio. He even took her past the tiny chapel and even tinier kiosk, which was open for just one hour each day. Finally, he pointed out the electrical plant room.

It was a relief to both of them when he finally announced, 'And now I must pick up Myrna. She'll be packed and waiting. Steve should be back before too long. Find someone to make you a coffee, and—'

'I can do coffee on my own, Terry,' Candace said gently. Several strands of his grey hair had fallen onto the wrong side of his parting, and he was rubbing his stomach as if he had heartburn. 'Just give Myrna my very best and have a safe trip.' She almost pushed Terry out through the administration entrance.

She had no trouble over the coffee. Found the nursing staffroom and was at once invited in. She hadn't finished her mug of unremarkable instant by the time Steve appeared in the doorway ten minutes later, but it didn't matter.

'Now, what do you need to get done?' he asked. 'Because I'm not seeing patients today, and you know Terry will have my guts for garters when he gets back if I haven't been looking after you.'

'He'll have your...what?'

'Guts for garters.' He grinned.

'That sounds violent.'

'So you'd better let me look after you, then, hadn't you?'

'Apparently!'

'Good decision.'

'Right, well, I need to get groceries, open a bank account and buy a car,' she announced.

Steve raised his eyebrows and grinned, appreciating the way she'd ticked off each item on her finger with such assurance. Perhaps he shouldn't have teased her with that piece of colourful Australian idiom just now. She didn't need him to entertain her so deliberately.

'Need to learn how to drive on the wrong side of the road, too?' he suggested.

'Well, yes.' Now she looked less confident, but the effect was just as attractive.

His expectations for the day notched themselves a little higher, and he was aware that they'd been high enough to begin with.

'I'll give you a driving lesson,' he offered.

OK, now she looked quite panicky. She gave a shriek, but she was smiling as widely as he was. 'This is going to be a treat for my fellow road-users!'

'Is that where we should start?' he asked. 'With the driving lesson? I can take you somewhere quiet first off then, when you've got some confidence, you can do the shuttling round to the bank and the supermarket. I'll just sit in the passenger seat and give a terrified hiss every now and then...'

'And slam your foot onto an imaginary brake pedal on the floor. I get the picture. Is it an automatic?'

'Yes, it is.'

'And is it insured?'

'Comprehensively.'

'OK, let's do it before I start thinking of excuses. How's the public transport around here?'

'Not good enough for commuting between three hospitals more than fifty kilometres apart, every week.'

'Thought not.'

So he gave her a driving lesson, and it wasn't nearly as hair-raising as either of them had feared.

I'm not flirting with her, Steve realised. Why is that? I'd planned to.

He had acquired some skill in this area over the years. He was nearly thirty-three, now. His brother Matt, three years his senior and married since the age of twenty-five, kept telling him, 'Get serious. Don't miss the boat. Stop going after women who have a use-by date.'

'Use-by date?'

'Like Agnetha. Women that you know are going to leave and let you off the hook. There was that other girl from Perth, too. Agnetha wasn't the first. Settle down!'

And he always found himself thinking, Yeah, obviously. Of course I will... I'm not a hardened bachelor. But not yet. Don't think I've quite come to grips with the married man's job description yet. When he took on a responsibility—and he was in no doubt that marriage was that—he liked to be sure it was one he was fully equipped to handle.

To prove to himself, and perhaps to Matt as well, that he hadn't missed the boat, be it kayak or cruise ship or ferry, he flirted with a variety of women. Mutually enjoyable. Nothing heavy-handed. Not threatening to anyone.

He kept it very light, never trespassed into the sorts of overtly sexual references and double meanings that he, along with most women, would have considered sleazy. He conceded that there was probably some truth to Matt's observation about women with a use-by date as well, although he didn't like the way his brother had worded it.

Candace Fletcher was only here for a year, and he was fully aware of the fact.

So perhaps this *is* flirting, he decided. We're laughing. Teasing each other a little. Only it's even lighter than usual, so I'm calling it something else.

Why?

Because I don't want to scare her off.

There was something in her eyes, something in the way she held that full, sensitive mouth. Coupled with the fact of her divorce, he was pretty certain that she would want a man to take things carefully, no matter how sudden and strong the spark was between them, no matter that she was leaving after a year.

Perhaps the spark was a little deceptive, too. They might both feel it, but that didn't mean acting on it would be a good idea. Some instinct told him to tread carefully, and to think before he acted in this case.

I didn't think twice with Agnetha, and neither did she...

The thought flashed through his mind and disappeared again.

They spent an hour on the quiet roads of Narralee's newest housing development before Candace announced that she was ready for downtown.

'Yes, I know you don't call it that,' she added.

'Just town will do.'

'Tell me how to get there.'

She parked without difficulty in the car park behind the bank and opened her account, then he showed her the supermarket nearest to Taylor's Beach and they tooled down the aisles with a big metal shopping trolley, which she filled to the brim.

Always an instructive experience, shopping with a woman for the first time. What secret vices did she display in the confectionery aisle? Did she actually cook, or merely reheat in the microwave? Agnetha had lived on rabbit food, Steve considered. Celery and nuts and carrots. Horse food, too. Various flaky things that looked and tasted like chaff.

Candace's diet held more promise and less obsessiveness. She smelled a rock melon—'canteloupe' she called it—with her eyes closed and a heaven-sent expression on her face. Then she put two of them in the trolley, right on top of the frozen chocolate cheesecake. She selected some delicate lamb cutlets and a medallion of pork, and they ended up lying next to the five-pack of lurid yellow chicken-flavoured two-minute noodle soups. She apparently drank hot chocolate, tea, three kinds of juice and four kinds of coffee.

He thought he'd been reasonably subtle in his analysis of her purchases, but he was

wrong. When they stood waiting at the check-
out, she tilted her head to one side and demanded, 'So, Doctor, how many points did I
lose? About fifty for the cheesecake and the
cookies, obviously, but I believe I do have all
the food groups represented in reasonable pro-
portion.'

'I wasn't—'

'You were, too! Silently analysing everything that went in the cart. Comparing me to—
well, to whoever.'

Agnetha. He almost said it, but managed to
stop himself. Felt colour rising into his neck
and thought in disbelief, My God, I'm *blush-
ing*!

'I thought so!' said Candace under her
breath.

It was a type of audition. She teetered on
the edge of resenting it. He had no right to
judge and draw conclusions like that!

Then, with more honesty and less bluster,
she decided that she was doing exactly the
same thing herself. Auditioning him for this
imaginary, unlikely affair she couldn't get out
of her head.

So far, he seemed like exactly the right candidate for such a thing, if she was going to
consider the question in such cold-blooded

terms. He would be easygoing, physical, fun to be with. He'd also possess certain shared understandings that didn't need talking about, because they worked in the same profession.

Yes, quite definitely an ideal candidate for an affair.

Is this what Mom was thinking about when she told me to go away? That I'd meet someone and have a crazy fling, get my socks sizzled off and come home as revitalised as if I'd been to a health spa for three months? That I'd be over Todd and Brittany? Dear God, *over* it. That it wouldn't hurt any more, and twist me up inside with bitterness and resentment and regret...?

The idea was both terrifying and dangerously alluring.

With her breathing shallower than usual, she asked, 'Are you sure there isn't anything else you need to do today? This is taking a long time.'

'My schedule's clear, so don't worry about it. Shall we take this lot home to your place and unpack it, then grab some lunch before we do the car?'

'Sandwiches? We have the makings for them now.'

'Yep. Great.'

They got to the first car dealership at two, after a lunch so quick and casual Candace might have been sharing it with Maddy. The salesman then spent half an hour addressing himself exclusively to Steve, even when it ought to have been quite clear to him that Candace was the prospective buyer.

'Do you think he realises why he didn't make a sale?' Steve asked her when they left.

She laughed. 'I handled it. In fact, it was useful. He talked to you while I had an uninterrupted chance to think about whether I really wanted the car.'

'I take it you didn't?'

She waggled her hand from side to side. 'Probably not. Let's keep looking.'

At the second and third dealerships, she test-drove two vehicles and finally decided on a compact European model, with very low mileage on the odometer. She felt exhilarated and slightly queasy at having parted with so much money so quickly. Still, it didn't make sense to delay. She was only here for a year. She needed to get organised, get her life sorted out, hit the ground running.

Did this apply to arranging a quick, therapeutic fling as well?

'Now you just have to drive it home,' Steve said, reminding her that in all spheres of life, actions had consequences.

'I don't know the way,' she answered.

'Which is why you'll follow me.'

By the time they reached home, it was late afternoon. Steve suggested an evening meal at a local Chinese restaurant, and that sounded fine.

Sounded fine.

In reality, it was harder. When someone was seated a yard away and facing in your direction, it wasn't as easy to avoid eye contact as it had been during driving lessons and grocery shopping. Candace drank a glass of red wine and regretted it. Jet-lag swamped her again, and the lighting in the restaurant was warm, inviting and intimate. She felt woozy, smily, relaxed and far too conscious of him.

When their eyes did meet, it was like tugging on a cord. She was a marionette and he was controlling the strings. He was making her nod and smile and listen with her chin cushioned in her palm and her elbow resting on the table.

'Hey, are you falling asleep?'

'No...'

'You will be soon. I'd better take you home.'

'You're making my decisions for me,' she retorted.

'Only tonight,' he said softly. 'Promise you, the rest of the decisions will be all yours.'

Perhaps he hadn't meant it to sound like such an intimate threat, but Candace panicked anyway. Her sleepiness vanished and she pulled herself to her feet, grating the legs of the chair on the restaurant's scratchy carpeting.

'Damn right they will!' she said, and saw his startled expression.

'Candace, I didn't mean— I *meant* it, OK?'

'I—I know. I'm sure you did.'

She turned away from him, felt his fingers slide in a quick, feather-light caress from her shoulder to her wrist, and was absolutely positive that she'd end up in his arms tonight. The idea was so breathtakingly terrifying that she didn't wait for him to pay for their meal. She simply stumbled out of the restaurant, hurried along the sidewalk and stood by the driver's side door of her new car until he caught up to her.

Steve didn't say anything about it. Not then. Not for the next few days. And he didn't kiss her.

He had more than one opportunity. Terry and his wife were still away, but the rest of Narralee's small medical community gathered to welcome her at a barbecue at Linda and Rob Gardner's on Saturday evening. She enjoyed meeting everyone, and laid some tentative foundations of friendship.

As Terry had predicted, Linda was going to be nice. She had a no-nonsense haircut, a chunky build, a throaty laugh and a wicked sense of humour. She was down to earth in her opinions, happy with her career and open in her love for her children and her even more down-to-earth husband.

Getting over her jet-lag, Candace stayed until ten o'clock and drove herself home, then saw Steve's car breeze past her house as she stood on the deck, watching the moonlight over the water.

He glanced across, saw her there, slowed down and waved. She almost wondered if he would come over. They'd had a long conversation at the barbecue. Lots of laughs in it, and some quiet moments, too. If he did come, she would offer him tea or coffee, while secretly quaking in her shoes...

But, no, he didn't show up.

The next morning, they met on the beach. Candace hadn't swum in the ocean in years, but loved it again at once. Taylor's Beach was patrolled and flagged in the Life-saving Association's colours of red and yellow, so she felt very safe swimming between the flags. Had no desire to go out as far as those surfers, though, in their slick black wetsuits.

One of the surfers was Steve.

She didn't recognise him until he came to shore with his creamy fibreglass board tucked under one arm, and he didn't see her until he'd put the board down, pulled his wetsuit to his waist and towelled himself.

He did this with rough energy, like a dog shaking off the water, then he caught sight of her, slung his towel over his shoulder and came over. Dropping her gaze, she was treated to the sight of his bare, tanned legs still dripping with water from the knees down, and his feet, lean and smooth and brown, covered with sand.

'Hi,' he said.

'You're not afraid of sharks out there?'

'Only when I see a fin.'

'You're joking, right?'

'We get dolphins here sometimes. They like surfing, too.'

'Now you're definitely joking!'

'No! Their bodies are perfect for it. They catch fish around here, too.'

'I'm going to look out for them. Still don't quite believe you…'

'You'll see them,' he predicted. 'If you spend any time on these beaches. The shape of their fin is different to a shark's, and so is the way they move in the water, but when you first glimpse one, before you've had time to work out whether it's shark or dolphin every hair stands up the way it does on a cornered cat. I tell you!' He laughed and shook his head. 'Yes, a couple of times I've been damned scared!'

He was still a little breathless. His hair stood on end and looked darker than it did when it was dry. The coarse plastic teeth of the zip on his wetsuit had pulled apart to just below his navel. She could tell by his six-pack of stomach muscles that he kept himself fit, and by his tan that he didn't always surf in his wetsuit.

My God, he's gorgeous! she thought, her insides twisting. Who am I kidding, that he'd want an affair? With *me*? Sitting here in my plain black suit. He'd probably flirt like this with my grandmother. Oh, I mean, was it even flirting? It was only friendliness. He was mak-

ing me welcome very nicely, as Terry would
have done, and I—Oh, lord, I'm so *raw*, right
now, I actually felt nourished by it. *Totally*
misunderstood it, obviously.

A girl in an extremely small orange bikini
wandered past. She was as blonde as natural
silk, sported a tan the colour of fresh nutmeg
and looked about twenty-five. For one crazy
moment, Candace was tempted to reach out,
haul her across by a bikini strap and park her
right in front of Steve.

Here you go. Much more suitable. My apol-
ogies for trespassing on your personal space
by even *contemplating* that you and I might
have—

'Ready for another dip?' he said. He had
taken no notice of the orange bikini, or the
body inside it, and now the girl had gone past.

'Um. Yes. Lovely.' Oh, hell! 'That would
be really nice.' She tried again, and managed
a more natural tone. 'I've been pretty timid on
my own, but it'd be great to get out beyond
the point where every wave dumps a bucket of
sand down my front.'

He laughed. 'OK, let's go.'

Then he reached for the plastic zipper and
peeled the wetsuit down even further.

He was wearing a swimsuit, of course. Board shorts, in fact. Black, with a blue panel on each side. Beneath the wetsuit, they'd ridden down below his hips. He had his back to her now, and she could see the shallow hollow just above the base of his spine. Like the rest of him, it was tanned to a warm bronze, and was dappled with tiny, sun-bleached hairs.

A moment later, he had hauled casually on the waistband and pulled the board shorts back to where they belonged.

They swam together for an hour, then she went home for lunch and he put his wetsuit back on and returned to the outer boundaries of the surf. She didn't see him when she went back to the beach for a walk late in the afternoon, didn't see him when she walked past his house on the return trip, although his car was in the driveway and a sprinkler was spinning round on the lawn.

Definitely, he was just being friendly.

And I appreciate that, she realised. Maybe that's the problem. I appreciate it, and I need it too much at the moment. I'd better get the rest of it under control.

Candace didn't see Steve again until Tuesday, when she had her first surgical list, consisting of three patients. Steve was scheduled to handle the anaesthesia.

She'd seen each of her patients the day before for a brief chat, and had gone through their reports from the pre-admission clinic. No danger signals. Chest X-rays and cardiograms all normal. Blood pressures within the acceptable range.

First was a scheduled gall-bladder removal on a fifty-three-year-old woman, followed by two straightforward hernia repairs, both on older men. Blood had been cross-matched for the gall-bladder patient as there was a higher risk of bleeding during this operation. All three of the patients were here on a day-patient basis. After the surgery, they'd make use of the 'political beds'—those reclining chairs that Terry had been so cynical about.

Preparing for surgery was like coming home. The OR—Theatre One, which sounded odd to her ears—was a place in which she was used to possessing undisputed control. She loved this environment, and the way everything was geared towards a single focus. One patient, one operation and six people who knew exactly what they were doing.

The scrub sinks were different—old-fashioned porcelain, with long levers on the faucets which you flicked on and off with a quick touch. She was used to stainless steel, and foot pedals. Theatre One had washable vinyl walls and the hard, antistatic floors which she knew only too well. They were murder on backs and legs after you'd been standing there for more than a couple of hours.

Candace was the last to scrub, and everything was ready to go now that she had arrived. She briefly greeted the other staff and the patient. Mrs Allenby looked a little nervous, of course. Years ago, Candace had had to fight the instinct to give her patients a reassuring pat, but now it was second nature to keep her gloved hands back.

There was music playing on a black compact disc player set up on a shelf. Something classical. Beethoven, Candace recognised. Not that it made any difference.

'Could we have that off, please?' she said.

The scout nurse, whose name badge was hidden beneath a green surgical gown, immediately went across and pressed a button on the player, bringing silence.

'Would you like something else, Dr Fletcher?' she offered. Her name was Pat, Candace found out a little later.

'No, thanks,' she answered, calm and polite. 'I can't operate with music.'

She registered one or two slightly surprised looks above pale green disposable masks, but didn't take the time to explain. This was her space now. All surgeons had their quirks, and she wasn't going to apologise for hers, now or later. She never swore or threw things or yelled at the nurses; she didn't practise her golf swing to warm up her hands; she was consistent in her preference of cat-gut length and instrument size.

But she liked silence. It helped her sense of focus. No music. A minimum of chatter. No jokes or ribbing. Absolutely no disparaging comments about the patient.

'OK, we're looking good at this end,' Steve said a few minutes later.

'Thanks, Dr Colton.'

Her gaze tangled with his as he looked briefly away from his monitors, and she could tell he was still thinking about the 'no music' thing. Maybe he'd chosen the Beethoven himself. Well, he could listen to Beethoven at home.

'All right, are we ready for the gas?' she asked, and began the operation.

She'd done it hundreds of times, probably.

Several litres of carbon dioxide were injected into the abdomen to provide a space to work in between the outer layers of tissue and the internal organs. A tiny incision allowed the passage of a laparoscope with an equally tiny camera on the end of it, manipulated by the assistant surgeon, Peter Moody. What the camera saw was then screened like a video, allowing Candace to guide her instruments. The lumpy, disorientating appearance of the human abdominal cavity on the screen was a familiar sight to her now.

This patient's symptoms suggested the need for a cholangiogram, which would confirm or rule out the presence of stones in the bile duct. In this case, the X-ray-type scan showed that, yes, there were three small stones present. Candace decided to remove them immediately, rather than bring Mrs Allenby back for a second procedure at a later date.

The monitors indicated that she was handling the anaesthesia well. Candace had no trouble in removing the stones successfully.

'If I know Mrs Allenby, she'll want to see those later,' Steve said.

'She's your patient?' Candace asked.

'Since I started here four years ago. And she's got a very enquiring mind, haven't you

Mrs A.?' Under anaesthesia, Mrs Allenby's conscious mind was almost certain to be unaware, but there was strong evidence that many patients could retain a memory of what happened during surgery. 'She wanted to know last week—' Steve began.

'Could we save it until later?' Candace cut in.

'Sure.' He gave a brief nod and a shrug.

Again, there was a moment of tension and adjustment amongst the other staff. Candace ignored it and kept going. She used tiny metal clips to close off the bile duct at the base of the gall bladder, as well as the vessel which provided its blood supply. Next, she used a cautery to detach the gall bladder from the liver, once again working through tiny incisions.

She brought the organ to the incision in Mrs Allenby's navel and emptied its contents through a drain. The gall bladder was limp now, and slid easily through the incision. She checked the area for bleeding and satisfied herself that all was looking good, then the patient's abdomen was drained of gas, the incisions were covered in small bandages, Steve reversed the anaesthesia and the operation was over.

Easy to describe, but it had still taken over two hours, and there was more work yet to be done. The two nurses chanted in chorus as they counted up instruments, sponges and gauze to make sure nothing was missing. Forceps and retractors clattered into metal bowls. Surgical drapes were bundled into linen bins. Mrs Allenby was wheeled, still unconscious, into the recovery annexe where two more nurses would monitor her breathing, consciousness, behaviour, blood pressure and pain as she emerged from anaesthesia.

The two hernia operations which came next were simpler and shorter. Both were of the type known as a direct inguinal hernia, which resulted from a weakness in the muscles in the groin area. A short incision just above the crease between thigh and abdomen on each patient allowed Candace to slip the bulging sac of internal tissue back into the abdominal cavity.

The first patient's abdominal wall had quite a large area of weakness, and Candace asked for a sheet of synthetic mesh to strengthen it. The second patient, several years younger, needed only a series of sutures in the abdominal tissue itself. Each incision was closed with sutures, and both patients would rest on the reclining chairs in the day-surgery room after their first hour or two of close monitoring in the recovery annexe.

She would check on them as soon as she had showered, Candace decided. You never came out of surgery feeling clean.

The shower beckoned strongly as she pulled off her gloves and mask just outside the door of Theatre One. Behind her, Steve and the other staff were preparing for a Caesarean, and Candace crossed paths with Linda Gardner. The obstetrician was about to squeeze in a lunch-break while Theatre One was tidied and replenished with equipment, ready for her to take over.

'Quiet in here today,' Linda commented.

'They'll probably appreciate a request for rock and roll, I expect,' Candace answered.

'So you're the culprit? You like reverent silence?'

'Reverence isn't a requirement,' she returned quickly. 'Silence is.'

'No one gave you a hard time?' Linda asked with a curious smile.

'In surgery, I don't give anyone the opportunity.' She softened the statement with a smile in return, then went and answered the clamouring of her aching back with a long, hot shower.

She emerged in a skirt, blouse and white coat twenty minutes later to find Theatre Two up and running and ready for her.

'All the symptoms of appendicitis, admitted through Emergency,' on-call theatre sister Lynn Baxter explained.

'Give me five minutes,' Candace said.

'And turn off the music?'

'Word travels fast around here. Thanks very much, yes.'

As usual, she didn't go on at length. Didn't admit either that the unexpected extension of her list today was almost as unwelcome as the discovery that the last leg of a long flight home would be indefinitely delayed. She considered it her responsibility to each patient and to the rest of the surgical team never to talk about how she felt.

No complaints, no explanations. Her aching back and feet were private—*her* problem. So were hunger, thirst and an itchy nose or a throbbing head.

And as for the inner turmoil she'd felt during each agonising step between her discovery of Todd's affair and their outwardly business-like divorce... She had said nothing about it at all until the final papers had been signed and their marital assets divided. Then she had simply made an announcement in the doctors' change-room at the end of a Friday list with a three-day weekend coming up. She had asked those present to pass the word around.

Most of her colleagues had been stunned, she knew, but they had three days to get used to the idea and to recognise the signals she was sending out. They knew her professional style by this time. Comments had been sympathetic and heartfelt, but mercifully brief...

Theatre Two was the exact twin of Theatre One, with all equipment and supplies set out in exactly the same way. This patient, a thirty-five-year-old woman with an uncomplicated medical history, had been given a pre-med through her drip and was already drowsy and relaxed, her considerable pain masked by the medication.

The appendix was notorious for sending out mixed signals, so Candace kept her mind open as she prepared to make the incision. You could open someone up and find nothing at all, even when a patient's white cell count was up and all his or her symptoms slotted into place. Or you could find—

'Good grief!' she said.

She'd spotted it before anyone else. There was a tumour wrapped around the appendix, turning this operation from a routine excision into a complex feat of surgical technique.

'It's huge,' muttered on-call assistant surgeon Mark Daley.

'But still potentially benign,' Candace said. 'We'll take it out straight away to send to Pathology, then explore a bit to see if there's any obvious spread to other organs.'

She excised both appendix and tumour, then looked at the ovaries, which were the most likely sites for a primary tumour in a woman of this age. Fortunately, they looked healthy and normal. Neither was there any evidence of metastasis to the liver.

'We're looking pretty hopeful on this one,' she concluded, and there was a sense of relief all round.

It was after three by the time Candace emerged from Theatre, and her stomach was aching sharply with hunger. She took another brief shower, grabbed a packet of potato chips from the vending machine in the emergency department, gulped some coffee and went straight in to check on the recovery of her day patients.

Mrs Allenby had eaten a sandwich and drunk some juice and tea, voided her bladder and shown a return of bowel sounds. She could manage a strong cough, her lungs were clear and she'd walked up and down the corridor a couple of times to assist her circulation.

'But my shoulder is hurting,' she said.

'Your right shoulder?'

'Yes.'

'Strangely enough, that's normal. Quite a common symptom. It's called referred pain, and that's really all you need to know about it, Mrs Allenby. It should go away on its own by the end of the day. You'll probably notice some discomfort from gas as well. Your stomach doesn't like being manhandled, and it may take a couple of days to settle down. But the surgery went very well, and I'm not anticipating any problems. Dr Colton would like to see you in his rooms in about a week to check on how you're doing.'

'I'll make an appointment.'

'Meanwhile, you can go home as soon as you're ready. You have someone to pick you up?'

'My husband's waiting.'

'Great! All the best, then. You were special, you know—my first patient in Australia.'

'Oh, how nice!'

Mrs Allenby went to the patients' change-room to dress, while Candace checked on her two hernia patients, who were both progressing normally but still too groggy to leave. As she slid her stethoscope around her neck, Candace heard Mrs Allenby say to a nurse, 'All right, I'm ready. Do I get my stones now?'

She hid a smile as she crossed to the three-bed recovery annexe where Andrea Johnson was just emerging from her anaesthesia. Steve had predicted his patient's interest in 'her stones'. In a relatively small community like this one, where a patient's GP could also be present during surgery, there would be more examples of this kind of knowledge. As Mrs Allenby had said in a different context, it was 'nice'. A difference for Candace to enjoy while she was here.

Andrea Johnson was still very sleepy and disorientated. She was lying on a wheeled hospital bed a few metres from the other patient in Recovery, the Caesarean delivery from Theatre One.

'Hurts,' was all she wanted to say. 'Feels awful.'

Candace ordered some additional pain relief, and out of the patient's earshot said to the recovery annexe sister, 'She's not ready to hear about what we found and what we did.'

'Wait until she goes upstairs?' Robyn Wallace suggested.

'Definitely. My notes are pretty clear, I think. I'll follow up in the morning and answer any questions she's come up with. If she seems too groggy to be told tonight, it can wait. And, of course, there'll be a wait anyway for the pathology results. Does she have family here?'

'No, she's single apparently. Drove herself in.'

'There must be *someone* to tell. Could you try and find out?'

'She was probably in too much pain to think about next of kin before.'

'That's usually when people want family or a friend around.'

'True.' Sister Wallace nodded.

'What have we got here? Two for the price of one?' said a new voice just behind them.

It was Steve. As anaesthetist, he was technically responsible for any complications in patients for the first twenty-four hours following their surgery, and he'd be taking a look at the two hernia patients as well as the Caesarean delivery he'd just been involved with.

Candace didn't understand his comment about two for the price of one. She assumed it was another Australian joke, but Sister Wallace looked blank as well.

'They're both my patients,' he explained. 'Sisters. And there's a whole posse of other Johnson and Calvert relatives upstairs, waiting to see Carina and the baby. Should probably warn you,' he added quietly to Sister Wallace, 'sparks will fly if they each realise the other is here. Andrea and Carina don't get on. Andrea seems to have cut herself off a bit lately.'

'I'll keep that in mind, and pull a curtain across,' Sister Wallace drawled.

'Speaking of getting on,' Candace said lightly, 'I'm heading *off*. It's been an interesting first day, but I'm done now.'

She should have known it wouldn't be that easy. Steve caught up to her as she reached her car.

'Heading straight home?'

'Yes, thanks to the existence of the frozen meals we picked up the other day, I don't need to stop for anything.'

'Frozen meals! Yum!' he drawled. 'How about steak instead?'

'Too hungry to wait for steak.'

'I'll get it on the grill as soon as I get home. Walk down to my place when you're ready, and we can call it a late lunch.'

'You don't have to.'

'I know. If I *had* to, I'd be chafing by now. Terry said, "Look after her till Monday."'

'Ah, so he *did* say that?'

She felt the severity in her expression. Couldn't always relax straight after surgery. He would probably think she was tight and humourless and no fun at all. From experience, however, she knew it would be worse to force a more laid-back mood. Wait until she got out of these cruel pantihose and unwound the stethoscope from her neck. She'd be far more relaxed then.

'Yes, he *did* say that,' Steve echoed steadily. 'But it's Tuesday now. This one's pleasure, not duty. And I'm such a crash-hot GP I can tell just by looking at you that your iron stores are low.'

Unexpectedly, she laughed. 'They probably are.'

'You need steak. And a swim.'

'The swim I won't argue with.'

'Neither will I, as long as it's *after* the steak.'

'All right...'

'Then, when we're sitting on the beach, I think we've got to talk about why you hesitated even for a second before you said yes to this,' he finished.

Casual tone. Meaningful after-shock.

It was a threat. Candace was in no doubt about that. And it was a threat which sent twin curls of panic and dizzy need spiralling wildly through her blood. She stalled the car three times on the way home.

CHAPTER THREE

THEY lay side by side on their towels in silence, soaking up some late afternoon sun and digesting what couldn't possibly have been called a late lunch.

Barbecued steak, a microwaved jacket potato and salad, dished up at a quarter to five? Not lunch. Delicious and satisfying, though. Steve Colton cooked steak very well.

He was going to ask me something, but I've forgotten what it was, Candace thought hazily.

She was too busy thinking about signals. Yes, *those* signals! The ones men sent to women, and the ones women, in their different way, sent back to men.

It's been so long... So long since I had to decide if I was imagining it or not. If I wanted it or not. If a man really meant it or not. I was so sure about all those questions the other day, but now...

Some men had flirted with her, had given off signals, during her marriage to Todd. They had been signals she had casually interpreted as meaning, If you weren't attached, I'd be interested. The key attitude on her part, of course, was 'casually'. She had never needed to test out her perceptions, to work out whether she was right or wrong.

Because of Todd, because of her marriage, it just hadn't *mattered*. She'd never had the remotest intention of responding to the possible, or probable, signals in any way. She'd never been tempted into an affair.

This time, it was different. A part of her craved the heady therapy of a successful fling. Another part of her was cynical, sceptical and just plain terrified. If I'm wrong... If I'm right, and it doesn't work...

If I'm sure I'm right, and I throw myself at him, and he laughs, or he's *kind*, or he tells me very carefully, Oh, but I'm married. Didn't you know? My wife is away visiting her parents for a week in Woggabiggabolliga—which seemed to be the name of at least half of the towns people mentioned around here, as far as she could work out.

Candace had to suppress a gulp of hysterical laughter at this point. Am I going crazy? Who knew that betrayal and divorce could do this to a person?

'You're different in surgery, aren't you?' Steve said suddenly, sitting up cross-legged on his towel and resting his elbows on his knees.

Candace immediately sat up, too. She didn't bother to argue his perception. 'Enough to be worthy of comment, apparently.'

'I didn't—'

'No, go ahead. It's OK.'

'I guess I thought you'd be more touchy-feely.'

'And instead I'm…?'

'You really give the impression that you know what you're doing and you know what you want.'

'Of course I do! I was doing this when you were still dissecting frogs, Steve!'

His abrupt launch into probing questions rattled her, especially the way it followed on from her own jittery train of thought.

'Don't,' he said.

'Don't what?'

'Don't pull rank.'

'Why not?' she retorted. 'I must be at least five years older than you.'

'Six, I think.'

'You've been checking?'

'Terry said you were thirty-nine.'

'Well, Terry is wrong! I'm only thirty-eight, and my birthday's not until July!'

They looked at each other and both laughed at the absurdity of her objection.

'Hey, can we start this again?' he said.

'Start what again?'

'Now you're being deliberately obtuse. This conversation. I hadn't intended it to get confrontational. I wanted to say that in surgery you were…' He hesitated.

'A royal pain about the music?'

'Yes, and it was great. I really liked the way you handled it. I *liked* you in surgery, Candace. I liked your focus and your confidence in the fact that it was your right to dictate the mood. But you were quiet about it. Polite.'

'I'm well brought up.'

'So well brought up that normally you're probably like most women and apologise when someone else steps on your toes, right?'

She laughed again, recognising the arrow-like accuracy of his observation. 'In my private life, yes. In surgery, Dr Colton, you'd better damn well apologise to *me*!'

He grinned and his blue eyes sparkled like the sun on the sea. 'Yep. I liked that. It was good,' he said, then repeated even more lazily, 'It was good.'

Seconds later, he was on his feet and reaching down to pull her up as well. 'Want to?' he said.

'A swim? Yes, I do.'

The surf was bigger today. 'Dumpers,' Steve told her. 'Be careful. They can flip you over pretty hard.'

He kept a careful eye on her and on the waves as they swam, and told her a couple of times, 'Not this one.'

After a while, she could feel the difference in the waves for herself. They didn't curl and pause and fold smoothly over today, but broke abruptly, like hands crashing on piano keys. If you caught them at the wrong moment, they sent you tumbling so that you emerged disorientated, with wrenched muscles.

'Where are the flags today?' she asked Steve.

'They don't patrol Taylor's Beach during the week, outside school holidays,' he said. 'We can stop, if you like.'

'No, I'm enjoying it.' And she felt very safe beside him, sensed that he really knew what he was doing in the water.

'Jump!' he interrupted, and they managed to keep their heads above water as a wave boiled around them. 'They're breaking all over the place. We'd have to go out a long way to avoid them.'

'No, thanks!'

They stuck it out for a little longer, then Candace got dumped again and came up with sand all through her hair and down her classic black one-piece swimsuit. Salt stung in her nose.

'Let's stop,' Steve suggested again, and this time she didn't argue.

They towelled themselves dry, and he slipped into a white T-shirt, while she wrapped a cotton skirt in tropical ocean colours around her waist, still enjoying the sun on the scooped back of her suit. They went for a walk, and explored the rock pools at the tide-level shelf jutting out from the headland at the southern end of the beach.

He showed her crimson and white anemones, glistening brown sea squirts and pinky-purple crabs. The late afternoon sun slanted golden on the water. A little later, a glorious sunset painted a palette of colour in the west, a mix of fiery orange, salmon pink and storm purple as clouds began to move across the sky.

The clouds hastened the onset of darkness and they turned back.

'I'll walk you home,' he said, and when they got there, he added helpfully, on a careless drawl, 'You can invite me in, if you like.'

'Are you hungry again?' she teased.

'We could have a drink on your deck.'

'You have a perfectly good deck of your own, Dr Colton.'

This time, he just looked at her. Silent. Patient. His blue eyes glinted and his mouth was tucked in at the corners. They both knew exactly what the other was thinking. It was a delicious yet stomach-churning feeling.

She sighed. 'Wine, beer, tea, coffee or juice?'

'Iced water?'

Out on the deck a few minutes later, he noticed her scratching her head. 'Hair still full of sand?'

'Yes, and when I try to get it loose, it runs down into my suit. Ugh!'

'We can do something about that, I think.'

He put down his clinking glass and disappeared inside, to emerge in a few moments flourishing her hairbrush. 'You were in a hurry this morning, weren't you?' he said.

'That's right. I left it on the table.'

'I noticed it earlier. Stand up and bend forward.'

'Um…'

'Let me. Please!' The teasing, knowing tone had gone from his voice suddenly, to be replaced by a husky note that was new. 'Please, let me. I'd really like to do it, Candace.'

She nodded, her throat too dry for speech. Time had slowed. There was an almost tangible sense of expectation hanging in the air. With her hands pressed on slightly bent knees, she faced him, then felt the light touch of his fingers on the back of her neck. A tingle flooded her spine.

Steve stroked the brush through her hair, his touch rhythmic and careful and slow. Cool, dry sand showered silently down onto her feet. Steve was silent, too. Only his fingers seemed to speak to her as they threaded a stray strand over her ear, then moved the thick mass to one side to brush in a different place. She was hypnotised by the gentleness of it, by the warmth of his touch and by the faint sound of his breathing. Could have let it go on forever.

'Now sit down,' he instructed her softly, 'And lean your head back.'

Her hair was like a cloud now, and the bristles of the brush tickled her temples and her scalp as he resumed his steady strokes. She closed her eyes and felt their lids flicker. She felt more vulnerable this way. The swimsuit wasn't outrageously revealing, but when she sat at this angle her breasts were thrust forward and she could feel the imprint of the cooling air pressing deep into the cleft between them. A shudder vibrated through her.

'You're cold,' he said. 'And I should stop. Don't want to.' He held her thick mass of hair in his hands like a rope. 'Could do this for ages.'

She opened her eyes and heard the brush clatter onto the glass-topped cane table. He knelt beside her. 'Your hair is gorgeous, and hidden underneath it are these stretches of soft skin I just want to kiss, Candace.'

He was doing it before he even finished talking about it, nuzzling her behind her ear, whispering his lips across her neck to reach her jawline, wrapping her hair loosely around his hands and using it to pull her close and find her mouth.

She gasped at the firmness and confidence and nutty sweetness of his lips. He released her hair so that it streamed over her shoulders and down her back, then brought his hands across her collarbone and down to brush lightly across her full breasts. They already ached.

Now he was pulling her to her feet and she went without hesitation, needing his strength against her body.

'Steve,' she murmured incoherently. 'Steve...'

'Mmm, you taste like the sea.'

'So do you. Salted peanuts, or something.'

'I could lick it off every inch of you.'

His hands rested lightly on her shoulders and his mouth tangled with hers, tongue and teeth and lips and tongue again. She felt as if this had been building between them for weeks or months instead of days, knew that her legs and mouth and hands were trembling.

'Every single inch,' he repeated, and slid the straps of her swimsuit from her shoulders, nuzzling at the salt on her neck as he peeled the straps lower with aching slowness.

Soon, soon, he would touch her breasts and feel just what this was doing to her. *Soon*...except that she couldn't wait another second. She arched her back and heard him groan with need as her fullness spilled into his hands.

He held her breasts almost reverently, lifted their generous weight in his hands then touched his lips to the swollen curves, drifting lower until he reached one throbbing nipple then moving across to the other. She flung her head to one side and gasped again, could have let it go on and on.

A car swished past on the road and a ragged thought entered her mind that anyone could have seen them here. Anyone could *still* see them. It was dark, cloudy now after that magnificent sunset, but all the same, if someone came along the sidewalk, looked up and saw their two shadowy figures and the tell-tale paleness of her bared flesh, that person would be in no doubt about what was happening up here on this open deck.

'Come inside,' Steve whispered. 'There are things I want to do to you that definitely aren't for public consumption.'

'I think you've already—'

'I know. It was so good. It's...' He broke off and his gaze swept down from her face to the pale, rounded shapes of her bared breasts, still heavy with need and tight against the chill of the air. 'Still very, very good.'

His hands drifted lightly up from her waist once more, whispered across her thrusting, pebble-hard nipples and came to rest on her shoulders. She was throbbing, on fire, desperate to touch him, too, in all the places that had drawn her unwilling gaze over the past few days. The hollow at the small of his back, his tanned shoulders, delicious backside, square jaw, steady mouth. But his touch on her sensitive skin seemed to paralyse her, and she couldn't find the will to move.

'Come inside now, *please*...' he whispered.

He didn't wait for her assent, just scooped one arm around her thighs and lifted her a step or two, then set her down again, locked her in his arms and almost dragged her to the bedroom.

Not that she was reluctant. Oh, no! But her legs were still shaky and half-numb. Her head just kept coming down to rest on his shoulder so she could press her mouth into the pad of muscle there, and taste the warring scents of salt and male skin.

The bedroom seemed too far away to wait for. There was a charge like an electric current between them and she wanted to pull off his clothes and wrap herself around him, claim him with her hands, feel his heat, hold him and never let go.

They barely made it to the bed, and were both far too impatient to take it slowly. He had come prepared for this. He had brought protection, and she didn't resent it. Of course he had come prepared! If she'd been a man she would have done the same. If she'd been a woman with more confidence in her own perceptions about their chemistry, she would have thought ahead and considered the issue herself.

So she was grateful for his forethought, in the twelve seconds she managed to give to the question, and then all of it—everything else in the entire world—became meaningless against the flood tide of their shared release.

They made love twice more that night. Candace was astonished at how rapidly their need for each other moved from being thoroughly sated to building to a conflagration once more. After the second time, they ate supper in bed—tall glasses of cold milk and that frozen chocolate cheesecake he had eyed in her shopping cart the previous week.

Then they went out and sprawled in each other's arms in the cane lounging chair on the deck for half an hour and talked. Silly stuff, not worth remembering or repeating. After midnight, after making love, it was hard to manage earth-shattering conversation.

It was lovely, though. Just…quietly… lovely. She wore nothing but a simple sarong knotted across her breasts and he had slipped back into his dry swim shorts. It became too cold eventually, so they had a giggly shower together to warm themselves up, and it led inevitably back to square one.

Finally, then, they slept until morning.

Morning.

The clouds had disappeared again overnight, and the day was already bright, even before seven. Candace had forgotten how strong the morning light was in this country. Glorious, she'd thought on other mornings. Today it seemed cruelly bright, and it hid nothing.

It probably didn't matter to Steve. He was still asleep, his body flung out in her bed as trusting as a child's. Almost as flawless as a child's, too. No crow's feet. No scars. No sags...

Candace fled to the bathroom for another shower and couldn't help pausing before the big mirror to take a merciless inventory of all she saw there. Hair like a bush. Creases around her mouth. And there was a mark on her left breast, a tiny bruise.

No, a love bite.

Hesitantly, she touched the spot with her fingers and remembered how Steve's lips and teeth had lingered there, and elsewhere, making her writhe. Today, it just looked like a bruise. Her breasts, with their nipples still darkened by the friction of Steve's mouth, seemed too heavy and large, too womanly, too pale. Hips and thighs as well.

'Lord, I need to lose weight!' she muttered, then laughed at herself. A few pounds, maybe, but that wasn't the problem.

The problem was that this body of hers was thirty-eight years old, not twenty-five, and the harsh Australian light would never let her forget it.

A rap sounded on the bathroom door, like someone casually tossing a handful of pebbles.

'Steve?' she questioned, cupping her hands instinctively over her breasts.

As if it could be anyone else! And as if there was any point in hiding this small segment of her nakedness from him!

'Can I open?'

'Uh...yes, fine.' She darted into the clear glass shower enclosure and turned the water on. It hid nothing.

'Hi...' he thwarted any attempt at conceal-ment straight away, opening the glass door and gazing at her '...gorgeous.'

Was that a nickname or a commentary? Whatever it was, she blushed darkly, happy and on edge at the same time.

'I have to head off,' he continued. 'I'm rostered to the emergency department today, and I've just been paged. Not totally urgent, but I'll have to cancel the full American breakfast.'

'Was I offering a full American...?'

'Sort of hoped you were,' he murmured, on a huskily suggestive note. 'But I'll see you tonight, OK?'

He reached confidently into the shower enclosure and pulled her close enough to kiss her wet face.

'No!'

The vehemence of it surprised both of them. Candace wrenched off the faucets, although most of her body was barely wet. She stepped quickly past him and reached for a towel. Lapping it around her body and holding it tightly in place, she left the bathroom. He followed her.

'Hey! Last night was great, wasn't it?' he said.

'Yes. Yes, it was.'

'Then what's the problem...hey, Candace?' The last two words were soft, sweet, like the way he'd spoken—those incoherent snatches of words—as they'd made love last night.

'You're m-making too many assumptions,' she stammered. 'Way too many. I'm not— We need to think about— If this is anything, it's just an affair, OK? And I don't want to take it—'

'Maybe I should just kiss you again, or something? That seemed to work pretty well yesterday.'

'*Work*? As a technique, you mean? A strategy for getting me to—?'

'*No!*'

It was his turn to rebel, and he did it more effectively than she had. He gripped her shoulders, tilted his head, brought his mouth to within an inch or two of hers. 'No, Candee,' he said softly.

'I *hate* that!'

'Candy?'

'Yes.'

'Not when I say it like this. Candee. Spelled double E. It's so sweet, can't you hear? And I mean it. Sweet Candee. Let me kiss you...'

'Mmm.' She turned her head away, pressed her mouth shut, but she was still in his arms and they were tight now, holding her, inviting her to lean on him. She could feel his heat, the elastic hardness of his muscles, the strong length of his bones beneath the fragrant skin she'd explored so thoroughly with her mouth and hands last night. The towel began to slip and, heaven help her, she no longer cared.

'Tell me it wasn't one of the best nights of your life,' he went on, his voice low. Its caressing lilt brought back flashes of memory—the intimate touch of his tongue, the power of his hips—making her shudder. 'Tell me we didn't light bonfires and set off rockets and make orchestras burst into symphony.'

'Yes, and it's wrong!' she retorted. 'I don't do that. I don't leap into bed with people...men...younger men...when I've only known them a week.'

'Less,' he pointed out.

'Less,' she agreed.

'So maybe it's time you did. Not *all* younger men, by any means. But me, definitely.'

'Why? *Why?*'

'Because it's good,' he said simply. He ran a finger lazily down from her throat to the top of the towel, which had slipped another three inches. Sensation stabbed deep within her. 'I thought it would be, and it is. I have to go.'

'Mmm.'

'Think about it, OK?'

She did. All day.

She thought about it in between seeing several of Terry's patients, as he was still in Sydney with Myrna. Terry's wife had had surgery yesterday—a lumpectomy and removal of the lymph nodes. She thought about it driving south on a winding highway through fragrant eucalyptus forests to Harpoon Bay. She had a surgical list scheduled there on Friday morning and wanted to make sure she knew the route and the hospital and staff a little. She thought about it driving north to Narralee again.

By the time Steve rang at six that evening, she was able to say at once, 'I'm sorry.'

'That's all right.'

'You see, I was married for nearly seventeen years and I didn't get a lot of practice at this and...' She stumbled to a halt.

'Am I seeing you, then?' he asked, as if this was all that mattered.

Maybe it was.

She took a deep breath. 'Yes. I'd like that. As long as there are no expectations. And as long as we keep it to ourselves. Strictly to ourselves.'

She didn't want anyone else judging or making assumptions.

'Yeah, I was going to say that, too. There are…reasons for that to be a good idea, aren't there?'

'Not that it's something I particularly—'

'Hey, let's not analyse it, Candace,' he said, his voice low. 'Not yet, anyway. Come over, and we'll have fish and chips on the beach.'

'Are you going to be at the hospital today?' Steve heard, at the other end of the phone. He recognized his brother Matt's voice.

It was seven on a Tuesday morning, a week after his first fabulous night with Candace. On Friday, she'd received the pathology report on Andrea Johnson's tumour and had phoned him to ask, 'Would you like to tell her, since she's your patient? It was benign. She should have no further problems at all.'

'That's great news, Candace! Yes, I'll tell her. Thanks for letting me know.'

'Well, you know, it's a real hardship for me to have to call you, Steve!' He loved that low suggestive note in her voice.

'Is that why we've both been doing it at least twice a day for the past forty-eight hours?' he'd answered her softly.

And, in fact, he'd expected this call to be Candace. To be honest, he was slightly irritable in his disappointment that it wasn't her voice he'd heard. Seven was early for his brother to be phoning.

'Yes, I'm rostered for surgery,' he answered Matt shortly, still not quite awake.

He could still smell Candace's sweet scent on his body. She hadn't stayed last night. Had left his place at one in the morning, with the imprint of her head on his pillow and his sheets tangled from the way she writhed at his touch. 'I really *have* to get some sleep, Steve!' she'd said, her voice low and husky with regret.

Just thinking about her—her responsiveness, the way her eyes went so wide and dark, the erotic charge that hit him every time he had his face in her hair, or touched the creases at the tops of her thighs, or held those fabulous breasts—made him throb with need. He wasn't yet trying to work out where this was going— Candace had mentioned the word 'affair' and he hadn't felt any need to challenge it—but he sure liked where it was at the moment!

'Might see you,' Matt said his voice a study in casual intonation.

Finally Steve woke up properly and the penny dropped.

'Hey, Helen's had the baby!' Steve's focus shifted at once, with a head-spinning wrench.

'No, not yet, but she's in serious labor, and it's pretty full on. Won't be long. We're heading for the car now. Her mother has just arrived to look after the big kids.'

Matt and Helen had a six-year-old son and twin daughters aged three, but still considered parenting a breeze and were ready for more.

'I'll try and drop in to see you, if things are quiet,' Steve promised.

'They won't be quiet at our end,' Matt answered. 'Helen's doubling up every two minutes now.'

'Get going, then, and I'll see you.'

He shook off the last vestiges of sleep—definitely hadn't been getting enough of it over the past few days, Candace was quite right— dived into his clothes, downed his cereal, skipped coffee altogether and left the house. Candace had a short list this morning, followed by Linda Gardner who had a couple of scheduled gynae procedures.

Sometimes there was a cancellation. A patient's pre-admission check-up might reveal a problem which made the surgery unsafe. Occasionally, some patients just didn't show up and had to be rescheduled for a later date.

This morning, Steve found himself hoping that something like this would happen.

Helen didn't have long labours, and he would be an uncle again before the scheduled list was completed. The sight of a sister-in-law he was very fond of and a brother he'd always been close to holding their much-wanted new-born baby was a pleasure he didn't want to put off for too long.

First, though, surgery with Candace at the helm…

I'm nervous, Candace realised as she scrubbed. When am I ever nervous before surgery? We're doing two vasectomies and stripping some varicose veins. Quick, simple procedures that I could do in my sleep. When am I *ever* nervous?

When the man I'm sleeping with—no, staying *awake* with, while we cling to each other and make all that wildness and ecstasy together—is behind one of those masks… That's when I'm nervous.

It had never happened to her before. Todd was a lawyer, her first and only sexual partner until last week, and their love-making had long since settled into the safe and predictable, well before his adultery with Brittany.

I can't bring this into the operating theatre with me. I hate distractions.

Even during the process of her separation and divorce, at least she'd never actually had to face Todd over the operating table. What if it was impossible?

Steve was already inside, gowned, capped and masked. All she could see were his eyes. So blue, so hot, so knowing. The patient was on the table, chattering and joking.

More nervous than I am? I don't think so!

'Hi,' Steve said to her. His tone was a caress, under the cover of some instructions from nurse to patient.

'Help me, OK?' Candace said. 'I'm—'

'You're fine. Come on.'

That was all. He just muttered the words, not even looking at her.

But at the familiar sound of his voice something clicked and shifted and she realised inwardly, Yes, of course I'm fine. I'm manufacturing a problem out of thin air, and there's no reason for it.

After this, the floor felt solid under her feet, the surgical instruments seemed to mould themselves to fit her hand and all three procedures ran as smooth as silk. She finished ahead of schedule. Linda's first gynae patient wasn't prepped yet, and Linda herself wasn't here.

'Great!' Steve announced to everyone. 'Because there's some action going on in the delivery suite today that I'm pretty interested in. My sister-in-law went into labour early this morning.'

There was a chorus of questions, but he shook his head. 'I'll tell you all about it when I get back, OK?'

The nurses, two friendly women in their fifties named Doreen Malvern and Pat Lister, began to prepare Theatre One for Linda's first procedure, while the previous patient was set up in Recovery with Robyn Wallace and Sue Smith. Candace filled in her notes and made a couple of phone calls, then Linda's patient arrived, drowsy from her pre-med and surrounded by snowy pillows.

'OK, now, one more lucky last time,' Doreen said. 'Janine, can you tell us your full name?'

'Janine Marie Prowse.'

'And your date of birth?'

'April the 18th, 1965.'

'And what are you having done here today?'

'My tubes tied.'

'Where's Dr Colton?' Candace heard Pat ask the anaesthesia nurse, Netta Robertson.

'Not back. I guess he's cluckier than we thought. But Linda's not here yet either.'

'On her way.' Robyn Wallace had just put down the phone. 'Five minutes, she says.'

'We'll start getting you set up, Janine, OK?'

'Where'd he go?' asked Joe Sheddin, the theatre orderly.

'Dr Colton? Up to Maternity. His brother's wife is having a baby.'

'Some drama was happening up there a little while ago,' Joe offered cheerfully.

'Yes, Helen Colton was having a baby,' Sister Wallace retorted.

She worked hard at keeping Joe in his place. Candace liked him, though. He wore his royal blue disposable cap like a pirate's head-scarf, low on his forehead, tilted slightly and knotted at the back, and he approached his job with unswerving good humour.

Cup of tea here or across the road? Candace mused to herself. She had some follow-up to do in the professional rooms she shared with Linda Gardner in the building across the street. No, I won't wait any longer here, she decided. I'll go across. I'm seeing Steve tonight anyway, so I'll hear all about the birth then.

She took a quick shower and changed, emerging to find Linda there, Steve still not back and everyone getting edgy. Then the heavy plastic swing doors that guarded the entrance to the theatre suite flapped open and there he was.

Grey-faced. Mouth like a thin chalk line.

'Steve…?' Linda began.

He just shook his head, grabbed some fresh shoe covers, a cap and a mask, all without a word. The phone on the desk in the recovery annexe rang.

'For you,' Sister Wallace said to Candace.

It was the receptionist at her rooms. 'Mrs Halligan has cancelled,' Gillian Thompson said. 'But there's a new referral on the waiting list. Shall I fit him in? He'll take longer than Mrs Halligan.'

'Remind me,' Candace said. 'Who's Mrs Halligan? And can you read me the referral letter?'

The new patient's medical problems were distracting and important enough to get her out of the hospital, and she spent a difficult afternoon in her rooms, her mind returning to Steve's pale face and his agonised silence every time she had a moment to spare. Finishing at half past four, she went straight home and left a stilted message on his machine.

'Am I still seeing you tonight? Obviously something's wrong. I'm praying it's not the baby, Steve.'

Then she cooked Bolognese sauce in case he hadn't eaten, and a chicken and rice soup because cooking the bolognese hadn't taken long enough. Foolish, probably. She didn't even know if he *liked* chicken soup.

He came up her front stairs at ten past six. Her heart jumped like a living creature inside her chest when she heard the rhythm of his footsteps on the resonant wooden treads. They went straight into each other's arms.

'What is it, Steve?'

'The baby died.'

'Oh, dear God…'

'It…he…it was a boy. He was born half an hour before I got there. Everything had been going fine, apparently. Helen didn't want a doctor, and there was no reason for her to have one. The midwife had it all under control. Then, when he was born… He had very severe Down's, and a malformed heart which just…didn't give anyone a chance. I'm thinking, you know, a hot-shot specialist and high-tech equipment but, no, realistically, no.

Wouldn't have made any difference. He only lived a few minutes.' His voice cracked. 'Poor Helen and Matt.'

He buried his face in her hair as if seeking nourishment and physical support.

'They must be devastated,' she whispered.

'Her mum brought the older kids in just now, while I was there. I went back as soon as Linda's list was done. I think that helped. The kids, I mean. They took photographs of him with everyone. They had him with them for quite a while. He looked...different, you know?'

'Yes...'

'But the twins didn't notice. They kissed him and talked to him and—Oh, God!'

He broke off and covered his face with his hands. Candace held him against her heart, and they talked about it for a long time. Helen hadn't had any prenatal tests, which was why no problem had been detected.

'She's a bit of an earth mother, and she's not thirty-five for another few months. There was no huge reason for her to have tests. The odds were in her favour,' Steve said. 'She's strong. Wonderful. They'll get through this.'

'Did you eat?'

'No. I mean, breakfast, a bit, but—'

'Do you want to?'

'I feel like I should be on hand, but they told me to go. Well, Matt and Helen need some time, just the two of them. The big kids have gone home with Helen's mother. Helen will go home tomorrow. Matt has to get back to work. He's an accountant...'

'Do you want to eat, Steve?'

'Hmm?'

'Let's eat, then go for a walk or something.' She was worried about how pale he still was, and if he hadn't eaten since breakfast...

He focused at last, let go of her, let out a huge sigh. 'Yeah... Yes, OK. Yes.'

'There's home-made chicken soup, or spaghetti Bolognese, or both.'

'You cooked?'

'I thought— You know— I knew something was wrong. Wanted to...' she spread her hands '...make chicken soup for you.'

'That's nice.' He smiled at last. 'I'll have chicken soup. Not all that hungry.'

After they'd eaten and talked some more, they both needed some air. Candace wasn't planning to leave Steve alone tonight until he asked her to.

The beach, in the darkness, felt good. They both left their shoes at home and just strode along the sand to the headland, with the in-coming tide teasing at their bare feet. Didn't say much. Not until they rounded the headland and went even further, to reach a tiny curve of sheltered beach.

Steve stopped and looked at it. It was deserted, lit faintly by moonlight, out of sight of any houses, with vistas stretching on down the coast, wild and beautiful.

'Do you know what?' he said, his tone grim and hungry and restless. 'I'm going to go for a swim.'

CHAPTER FOUR

STEVE began to pull his shirt over his head before Candace could even reply. The ocean scared her a little at night, despite the way the moon silvered the white foam so prettily.

'I'm coming, too.' The words broke from her lips before she could think twice about saying them.

He turned back to her and grinned. 'I hoped you would.'

He peeled down his baggy shorts, taking his underwear with them.

'Oh, like that?'

'Or we'll have to walk back wet,' he pointed out. 'And we haven't got towels.'

'True.'

'A couple of other advantages I can think of as well...'

He watched her as she slipped her sea-blue washable silk shell blouse over her head, unfastened her gauzy sarong and unclipped a black lace bra. Their clothing littered the sand, and she felt a flutter of vulnerability. About her nakedness. About his gaze.

It soon disappeared. He took her hand and pulled her towards the water. The waves were gentle tonight, like sheets of silver fabric slipping in and out. It was cold at first, but Steve wouldn't let her take things slowly.

He ran, still dragging on her hand, and she knew he needed the release of a sudden plunge so she went with him until she lost her footing at waist depth.

They jumped and dived, undulating like dolphins, floated on their backs, trod water, let the waves sweep them closer to shore and then waded out again, past their thighs. Hardly spoke at all. It must have been ten minutes or more before he took her in his arms, his face dark and serious.

'Thank you,' he said. 'I needed you tonight.'

He pulled her close, so that she could feel the sea-chilled wall of his chest against her breasts and, a moment later, his mouth on hers. Her response was as immediate and powerful as ever. As they kissed, her hands curved on his hips and slid back to his taut behind, anchoring his growing arousal against her. He groaned, dragged his mouth from hers and buried his face in her neck.

She arched her back convulsively, her body openly begging for the touch of his lips on her throat and her nipples. The ocean washed around them, contrasting the coolness of its caress with their own increasing heat.

'Can we go home?' he muttered at last.

'That far?' Her arms were wrapped around his neck now. 'The dry sand is only a few metres away. No one's here. We could find a hollow between those small dunes...'

Candace was shocked at the words the moment she'd uttered them. She had never conceived of anything so impulsive, impatient and wild.

Steve's hands trembled as his arms wrapped tightly around her once more. 'Oh, lord, Candace, I'd love to,' he breathed, warming her neck. 'I'd *love* to!'

They clung to each other as they stumbled up the sand, stopping several times to kiss, each time with greater need. The low dunes just ahead seemed expressly shaped for what they wanted.

'Wait until we're dry,' Steve said wickedly, and kept her on her feet, driving her rapidly mad with longing as he caressed her.

Finally, they sank into the cupped hand of the hollow and pushed each other over the edge of explosive release within minutes.

The sand was cool. A little scratchy, too, a little sticky. It didn't seem to matter. They lay there, listening to the ocean, listening to the beat of each other's hearts.

'I've never done this before,' Steve said.

'No?' She lifted herself onto her elbows, her face betraying her surprise as she leaned over his body and looked into his eyes.

'Why, have you?' he asked.

'No, I haven't, but...that's different. I've only lived near this beach for ten days.'

'Implying that I've lost a lifetime of opportunity?'

'No, I'm glad it was a first for you, too, Steve,' she replied almost shyly. 'Very glad. Because it was...'

'Incredible, wasn't it?' He sounded shy about it, too.

'Mmm, incredible.'

'Totally...' He kissed her softly, caressed her a little, then dragged his hands reluctantly from her body. 'Twice, though, would be a bit too sandy.'

'Mmm, I think so.'

He sat up, grabbed her hand and began to stand. 'Let's get our— Ah, *shoot*!'

'What?' She followed his gaze towards the water, just in time to see the faint dark shape of a piece of clothing sweep up the beach on the lacy edge of a wave and come to rest on the sand. 'Oh, no! Our clothes!'

'Tide's coming in,' he agreed. He had already started down the beach. 'I can see one, two...only two things. Hell, I hope one of them's my shorts, because my keys are in the pocket!'

He broke into a run, seized the sandy, sodden garment, then lunged for another one several yards off. 'My keys are still there, and this is your skirt.'

'Surely we can find the rest if we look,' she said. 'My bra, and—'

'Hang on.' He lunged for another dark shape in the water, and pulled up a skein of seaweed.

'Well, I'm not wearing that!'

Suddenly, they were both laughing.

'This is so crazy!' he said.

'Keep looking!'

'I think you'd look pretty good in seaweed.'

'Yeah, right!' she drawled.

'Seriously, like a mermaid. Your hair is rippling all down your back. Knot that sarong at your waist like a mermaid's tail, and—'

'OK, so where does the seaweed go?'

'Across your breasts, draped like a scarf and offering tantalising glimpses of—'

'*Keep looking*, Steve!'

But it was no use. They looked, stooped down and felt around in the moving water for several more minutes, found two more bunches of seaweed but nothing made of fabric, and finally accepted that the rest of their clothing was lost to the depths of the Pacific.

'Could be worse,' Steve pointed out.

'Could be,' she agreed cautiously. 'You'll be quite decent, for a man. Easier for men!'

'And my mermaid fantasy will come true.'

'Read my lips. I am *not* wearing the sea-weed!'

'Spoilsport! OK, let's see what we can do instead.'

He took the gauzy sarong, squeezed out as much water as he could and wrapped the clinging garment around her, knotting it above her breasts. His knuckles grazed Candace's cold-hardened nipples through the wet fabric as he completed the task. The garment clung like a second skin and hid little.

'Steve, I can't…!'

'No choice, sweetheart.'

'What am I going to do?'

'You mean, what am *I* going to do? Put my arms around you to keep you warm. One around your shoulders, like this, and one across your body, like this, and even if we do meet an unexpected crowd of midnight life-savers or something, no one will see a thing…'

My heaven, if Todd could see me now! she thought, as they wandered past the dark, rocky headland together and back to a deserted Taylor's Beach. Walking in a wet, near-transparent sarong along a beach late at night with my handsome lover's body shielding and warming mine, after we've pleasured each other in the dunes beneath the moonlight.

I wish he *could* see it! Oh, damn, I *wish* he could see me *right now*! came the bitter inner realisation.

All those things he accused me of in the weeks before he finally left. That I was stale. Not that our marriage was stale, but *me*. That I was stifling him, boring him, dragging him down, making him feel old, so that the whole thing became my fault and it was clear he didn't even want to *try* and save what we once had. What I *thought* we once had.

Well, I'm not 'stale'. It wasn't just me, and my fault, and if he could see this now… Oh, if he could see it…

'There, you see,' Steve said softly, holding her close in his arms just outside her front door. The wet fabric had chilled her, despite the shelter he had given her, and she shivered. 'Quite safe. No one saw a thing, and I got to hold you against me all that way.'

'Mmm, it was nice,' she agreed.

'Much better than nice.'

'Do you…uh…want to come in?' She bent down and got her key out from beneath a flower-pot.

'I won't,' he said soberly. 'I'm going to drop in at the hospital, have a talk to the night sister in Maternity and hear how Helen's been doing. Matt will be at home now, probably. He would have wanted to help Helen's mother with Jake and the girls. If Helen's still awake I might sit with her for a bit, too, if she wants some company.'

Candace nodded silently and Steve made a gesture of helplessness. It was clear that he wished there was more he could do.

'You're close to Matt, aren't you?' she observed softly.

'To Helen and Matt,' he agreed. 'Especially since our parents died. But…you know… Aussie males.'

'I'm beginning to…'

'We're not— We don't talk to each other about the real stuff much. I was all prepared to go in there today and punch him in the arm and make some stupid joke about breaking out the cigars. With this, all I can think of is being there, giving them some of my time.'

'That's more important than words, Steve. I'd offer to come with you, only I'm sure she doesn't need any more strangers.'

She opened the front door and stepped inside.

Leaning against the doorjamb, he murmured, 'Let me kiss you one more time?'

And she couldn't help leaning forward to meet the brush of his lips. 'Tell Helen and Matt that my thoughts and prayers are with them.'

'I will.' He nodded. 'Night, Candee.'

'Night, Steve.'

In the shower a few minutes later, washing off the sand and salt, she felt exhausted and churned up inside. Happy, confused, sad about Steve's tiny nephew, physically sated yet miles from sleep.

Miles from sleep. She went to bed at eleven-thirty, was still awake at one, then finally dropped into a dark, heavy slumber a little later, only to be shattered into wakefulness again by the sound of the phone when her bedside alarm read 2.05.

Her first thought was Steve, then Helen, the baby, the beach, their missing clothes... Finally, reality crystallised into focus as she recognised her daughter's voice.

'Mom? You sound like you were *asleep*!'

'I was,' she croaked. 'It's two in the morning here.'

'No, it isn't! It's supposed to be six in the evening. Grammy and I worked it out.'

'Oh, you're at Grammy's?'

'Yeah, and she said the time in Australia was sixteen hours behind.'

Typical of Elaine West, founder of West Interiors, one of the most successful interior design firms in Massachusetts. It wouldn't occur to her that Boston could be behind anyone in anything.

'We're sixteen hours *ahead* here, honey,' Candace sighed. 'I promise you, it's two in the morning. How come you're at Grammy's on a school day?' Mom usually saved Maddy's frequent overnight visits for weekends.

'Dad said I could cut classes today. He dropped me off on the way to the hospital. Brittany's had the baby, a week early. Six o'clock this morning. Dad just called, and he wanted me to let you know. Everything went perfect, yada, yada. Weighed eight and a half pounds, and they've named him Luke.'

'You don't sound too thrilled,' Candace said cautiously.

'Oh, I will be when I see him.' Maddy's prediction was blithe. 'I'll go nuts over him. My baby brother! But I mean, like, it's kind of complicated, you know? Brittany…just kills me most of the time.'

There was an uneasy pause, then Maddy retreated quickly to safer ground. 'I'm real sorry I woke you up, Mom.'

'It doesn't matter.' Candace made a huge effort. 'Tell me how everything else is going.'

They talked for ten minutes, then Elaine came on the line to threaten, 'I'm not buying a gift for that baby! I'll send flowers and a card on your behalf—since I *know* you'll feel it's the right thing.'

'It is the right thing, Mom. Like it or not, this is Maddy's brother.'

'You're right. It is,' Elaine agreed. 'You're too generous for your own good. I've brought you up very well.' The contradiction between these two adjacent statements didn't seem to trouble her.

'You know, I'm surprisingly fond of you, you strange creature,' Candace interposed, after a short laugh.

'But I will *not* send a gift of my own!'

'No one is saying you have to, Mother.'

'No, well, in case you were planning on telling me I had to, I'm getting in first and telling you I'm not!'

'Thank you for your support.'

'Are you handling it, darling?'

'Yes, I'm—' Candace broke off to control a jerky breath. 'I'm handling it. Something—'

She stopped again.

Something else happened today. Another baby was born, and didn't live.

A thought…a wish, so dark and horrible that she didn't even frame it into words, flooded her mind, and she felt sick. She gave a strangled sound.

'I beg your pardon, Candy?'

'Nothing,' she said quickly. 'I…should go. I need to get back to sleep.'

'I just can't believe that. You're really sure you're *ahead*?'

'I'm quite sure, Mother, dear!'

But when she put down the phone, she didn't even try to sleep again straight away. Got restlessly out of bed instead, wrapped herself in a heavy cotton kimono and went out onto the deck, needing the air and the darkness.

Did I really think it, even for a second? That it should have been Todd's baby that died...? That it would serve him and Brittany right for their betrayal? Oh, lord, what's happening to me?

She buried her face in her hands and recalled that night's earlier thoughts about Todd with stark clarity as well.

I wanted him to know that Steve and I had made love on the beach. I wanted to throw it in his face like a handful of sand and watch him grimace in pain and jealousy. That's *wrong*!

Maybe it was human and normal, but it was still wrong, for more reasons than she could get straight in her head right now.

It underlined her vulnerability, for a start. She wasn't over Todd, if she could fantasise about punishing him like that. Could a new relationship hasten the healing process or, more likely, would it only deepen the wound that the end of her marriage had made?

How realistic was it to believe that she wouldn't get hurt again? Steve was a young, good-looking man who might be the town's most notorious womanizer, for all she knew. Telling herself that she only wanted an affair—and meaning it—wasn't necessarily a protection.

And, finally, feeling like this about Todd was impossibly unfair to Steve.

Images of her ex-husband taunted her. Memories of how he'd held Maddy as a newborn, how he'd whispered his pride to Candace, spoiled her with presents and flowers, champagne and chocolates and jewellery. He'd been smug about his virility, and she'd found that endearing at the time.

Now, at this very moment, on the far side of the world, he was lavishing all these things—and more—on another woman and her newborn son.

It's so, so unfair to Steve. I'm using him. Like a weapon. A revenge strategy. A knife in Todd's back. Which is laughable, because Todd will never even know.

Taking Todd out of the equation, then, she was left with herself and Steve. His needs, and hers. His feelings, her vulnerability.

I can't go on with this. My motives are too ugly, and I don't like to feel them in myself. I'm scared. I'm not ready. I'll have to tell him.

I should have realised it and fought this whole thing much harder from the beginning.

Candace didn't tell Steve of her decision for some days, hanging back out of consideration for Helen and Matt, and Steve's involvement in their tragedy.

Little Robbie's funeral took place on Thursday morning, and Steve took six-year-old Jake and the three-year-old twins, Claire and Annabelle, for the rest of the day to give their grieving parents some time alone.

On Friday the family went for a picnic, while Steve and Helen's mother, Barbara, boxed away the baby clothes, the little plastic bath, the bassinet and the snowy pile of nappies.

Candace knew all this because Steve came over on Friday evening and told her, pacing her living room restlessly, his sentences jagged and broken. They discussed a couple of patients as well, over a beer and a bowl of corn chips, but when he leaned against the doorway to the deck and started talking about going somewhere for a meal and then back to his place, she knew it was time to speak.

'I can't, Steve. I—It's best not.'

'Not?' He looked up, startled, his blue eyes suddenly bright with suspicion.

'Best that we don't go on with this.'

Silence, then, 'That's a…development, let's say.'

He circled closer, bringing his gorgeous body into the range of her awareness. She was distracted by it. He must have showered before coming here, because the hair at the back of his head, just touching his neck, was still damp.

She wanted to thread her fingers through it and fluff it dry. His T-shirt was untucked a little, bunched near that hollow in the small of his back which she loved to caress.

She felt a tightness clamp around her throat, and a pull like a magnet between them. Awkwardly, she stepped sideways to stand behind the two-seater couch. It created a barrier which she needed.

What can I say? What excuses can I come up with?

The truth. That was the only fair thing. There had been such honesty in the way they had responded to each other. Honesty in every touch of skin on skin, and in the tumultuous climaxes they'd shared. She couldn't start lying to him now.

'I realised…that this was too much about my feelings towards Todd,' she said carefully. 'It was about showing him that he wasn't the only one who could launch into some wild, sizzling—'

'You *told* him about us?'

'No!' She wrung her hands. 'Of course not! The showing-him thing was all in my head. You know, "Success is the best revenge." Who said that?' she demanded distractedly.

'Ivana Trump, I think,' he drawled, his tone careful and hard to read.

She gave a short laugh. 'There! Exactly! Another wife who lost her husband to a younger woman. I can't—I'm not going to do it. Not to you. Not to myself. We both deserve better.'

'Better? I thought the other night on the beach was pretty good,' he said, deadpan.

'Yes. It was. It was fabulous. And all the way home, I kept thinking that I wished I had *photographs*. *Proof* of how good it was. So that maybe one day when I went back, I could carelessly leave them lying around on my coffee-table. Oh, nothing flagrant. Not really pictures of what happened in the dunes. But just of you and me standing on the beach in the sun, in our swimsuits, with our arms around each other, laughing.'

'I'll go home and get my camera right now...'

She ignored him. 'And Todd would find them. Or Brittany.' She pressed her palms against her eyes. 'That's...just horrible.'

He was silent, and she blurted after a moment, 'See!'

'See what?'

'See, you're repulsed.'

'I'm not.'

'You *should* be!'

'You didn't do it, though, did you?' he pointed out. He was still watching her carefully. 'And you don't intend to do it. Not really. You just fantasised about it. There's an awful long way to travel between the two.'

'I *wanted* to do it.'

'And then you thought better of it.'

'I was using you,' she insisted.

She heard the hiss of his breath between his clenched teeth and an impatient mutter, low in his throat, that she couldn't understand. There was another beat of silence, then he said, his voice rising, 'Yes. OK. Maybe you were.'

He was still moving restlessly through the room, but his body was far more angular now.

She was aware of his strength, the full force of his personality, the driving certainty of his mind.

'What can I say, Candace?' he demanded. 'That I liked being used? That you should feel free to use me that way any time you like? No! It doesn't sit well, does it? You're quite right, there. Or I could argue that there was a lot more to it than that. A hell of a lot more. There *was*, and that's what's important. And I thought you might have had the courage to see it.'

'Courage? This is taking courage! To admit the truth to you about my motivations.'

'Part of the truth, Candace. One very small part.'

'Steve—'

'Stop, OK?' His jaw was hard and square. 'Have it the way you want it. It's over. I liked it while it lasted.'

'Yes, yes, so did I,' she agreed, hardly knowing what an admission it was.

Steve's voice softened again. 'The plea-sure…and the need…whatever its source…wasn't all on one side by any means, Candace.'

'No. I—I know.'

He watched her for a little longer, and she felt her skin heat up and begin to tingle. 'No hard feelings,' he drawled.

'Thank you,' she answered, while wondering if he really meant it.

'And I'm still here if you need help with anything,' he offered. It was the kind of thing a man like Steve Colton would say, she guessed. Obligation more than anything else. 'I'm on call in emergency this weekend, but—'

'Terry's back this weekend,' she cut in.

'Terry doesn't have quite the same things to offer that I do.'

The threat was blatant, seductive and unwanted, all at the same time. Memories and images of the things he had to offer came flooding into her mind. The things he had offered and that she had accepted, giving them back in double measure, finding a passion within herself that she hadn't known she possessed.

Proving something. Showing off. Lashing out at Todd. Not in control of what was happening at all.

'If you're saying that it isn't over,' she blurted, 'you're wrong.'

This time he didn't argue, just said softly, 'See you around, Dr Fletcher.' And let himself out of her house.

CHAPTER FIVE

'How were they breaking on the weekend, Dr Colton?' Joe Sheddin asked.

He was wheeling in Candace Fletcher's second patient for the morning. It was another Tuesday, and the visiting American surgeon's fourth surgical list at this hospital since she'd started work here.

'They were breaking like a dream, Joe,' Steve answered the orderly. 'But it didn't do me any good. I was on call in A and E, second weekend in a row, and we were pretty busy. Ended up sending a few patients elsewhere, including one to Sydney and two to Canberra.'

He could see Candace through the open doorway of Theatre One. She was on the phone and had a pen in her hand, hovering over some notes. Her hair was folded up onto her head in a thick pile that immediately made him want to thread his fingers through it and pull it down.

Their relationship hung at a balance point that tortured him at the moment. He knew...every nerve-ending in his body knew…that she wanted him as much as he wanted her, and soon, very soon, he planned to challenge her determination to resist his pull on her senses.

Not yet, he'd told himself for days now. Try it too soon, and you'll be back to square one. Another pointless argument about her ex-husband. She's not ready yet. But very soon…

Ending her phone call to a doctor in Harpoon Bay, Candace put down her notes and went to scrub, listening to the conversation between the nurses with half an ear.

'Oh, but I don't swim after the end of March,' Doreen was saying.

'That's crazy! It's the best time of year for swimming, Doreen, really it is!' Pat answered.

Was it Candace's imagination or was everyone getting more chatty? They had gotten used to her, and she had gotten used to the relaxed atmosphere and the friendliness of the staff. Her habit of formality, focus and silence in the OR was beginning to break down.

Or perhaps it's because of Steve…

For various reasons, setting up a regular Tuesday list in Narralee was working well for Candace. She then alternated surgery in Harpoon Bay and Shoalwater on Fridays, leaving the rest of the week clear for pre-admission and follow-up appointments, and the occasional emergency call. Since Steve's regular anaesthesia day was Tuesday, they saw each other in Theatre every week.

Saw each other? That was a very weak phrasing. Their gazes clashed and clung over their masks. Their bodies pulled together like magnets. Even the sound of his clothing shifting against his skin drew the straining attention of her ears. And every casual exchange between them was laced with a golden thread of deeper meaning.

She hadn't expected their working relationship to develop in this direction after she'd put the brakes on their affair. She'd expected tension. Brittle, hostile, unpleasant tension, and lots of it. But it wasn't like that. He had an aura of wicked and knowing awareness about him every time he looked at her or spoke to her and…yes…OK, *that* was why the mood in Theatre had changed.

She found herself chatting to the other staff to break the tautly stretched fibres of her own awareness. She didn't want him to guess how often or how strongly she found herself reliving that night on the beach. Their other nights together, too.

'Can you count for me, Eric?' Steve asked their patient. 'Backwards from a hundred, OK?'

'Right, sure.' Eric nodded. 'A hundred, ninety-nine, ninety-eight, ninety-seven...'

Seconds later, he was out. Steve checked his monitors. Pat wheeled a trolley closer to the table.

This was another gall bladder removal. The patient was forty-eight years old and in good general health. Past abdominal surgery and consequent scarring had made him an unsuitable candidate for laparoscopic surgery, so Candace was taking the traditional route, opening up the abdomen with a long incision.

It would necessitate a longer hospital stay, more painful recovery and more protracted convalescence, but in this case there was no choice.

'Come with me to the sea pool by the harbour one day, Doreen,' Pat said, as the team began its work.

They were still talking about swimming. Mr Kellett's abdomen was already stained a rusty red from its generous swabbing with antiseptic.

'I didn't know there was a sea pool,' Candace came in. 'Scalpel, Doreen. Is it natural, or...?'

She made a clean incision, working with the lines of his previous scarring as far as possible.

'No, it's a proper Olympic-sized pool,' Pat explained. 'But it gets topped up by the incoming tide twice a day, and then it partly drains when the tide goes out, so the water's always fresh.'

'Fresh salt water? Bit of a...what's the word?'

'Oxymoron?' Steve supplied.

'That's it,' Candace agreed. More scarring and adhesions were showing up now that she'd reached the abdominal cavity. He'd had a serious accident several years ago, and some impressive surgery to repair the damage. 'Gauze...no...yes, Peter, thanks, a bit closer, here.'

'Fresh,' Pat repeated firmly. 'Because there's no chlorine. It's lovely.'

'Freezing!' Doreen said, unconvinced.

'You don't notice it after a few minutes.'

They couldn't reach an agreement on the subject, and continued to bat it around as the operation proceeded uneventfully. There was a three-way split between the five locals. Steve and Pat were firm believers in year-round ocean bathing, whether in pool or surf. Doreen and Netta Robertson, assisting Steve with anaesthesia, were unimpressed with the sea pool. Assisting surgeon Peter Moody, holding a retractor in place, admitted that he could be coaxed into it in the right mood, even in July.

'But I wouldn't make a habit of it,' he said.

Candace felt that she didn't have enough data to go on.

'I haven't been here in July,' she said.

OK, here was the gall bladder, right where it should be, and she could feel through the fine latex of her gloves exactly why it needed to come out. Several stones in the common bile duct, and more in the gall bladder itself. If they stayed there, they often didn't cause major problems, but once they moved into the ducts, it was a different story. This patient had complained of pain and nausea, and had recently been treated for an infection. The organ was overdue for removal.

'I'll take you for an early morning dip in the sea pool one day soon,' Steve promised lazily. 'And you can see what you think.'

'And I'll come and watch, wrapped up in a big, thick coat,' Doreen said.

'Yeah, and I'll sneak up behind you and push you in,' he threatened.

Candace laughed...stones were coming out nicely...and felt that syrupy sense of delight that always washed through her when Steve had a smile in his voice.

'We've got his temp climbing a bit here,' he muttered. The smile had gone. 'Thirty-nine point three.'

'OK, thanks,' she replied. The duct was clear now.

'Everything else is fine.'

'I'm tying off the duct. We're making progress.' She continued to work, closing off the duct and the blood vessel at the base of the gall bladder. She wasn't particularly concerned about Steve's report. Her thought train juggled two completely different subjects at once.

Am I going to go for that swim in the sea pool with Steve? Need the cautery for this vessel… It's tempting. That's got it. No more bleeding… He makes me flutter inside, and he knows it. Blood's looking a bit dark.

'Steve, how's his oxygen reading?' she asked casually.

'Good. Normal.' Their eyes met for a fraction of a second above their masks.

Does he think he's just biding his time, or something? Oh, hell, admit it, maybe he is. Yes, he is. I feel like we're both waiting for something to happen, for it all to start up again.

The idea beckoned so powerfully that she was swamped with the sudden heat of desire.

'Temp's over forty, now. That's a steady rise,' Steve said.

'He's getting very sweaty,' Doreen commented.

'Blood pressure, too,' Steve said. 'It was 90/60 a minute or two ago, now it's jumped to 124/85.'

'Dark blood,' Candace said.

'Temp's still coming up, and his heart rate is climbing, too.'

'His hands are mottled.' Another observation from Doreen.

'You've got dantrolene here, right?' Candace demanded urgently. 'Dantrolene sodium? Of course you have!'

Pat went through the swing doors of the operating theatre at a run.

'Malignant hyperthermia?' Steve said. 'Hell, is that what's happening?'

Suddenly, the relaxed atmosphere shattered into a thousand pieces.

'Has to be,' Candace said. 'How's his temp now?'

'Over 41.'

They all knew what malignant hyperthermia was, although it was rare. Most commonly, it was an inherited trait, a susceptibility to certain anaesthetic agents which resulted in rapid temperature elevation and usually hypertonicity— rigid muscle tone—as well. It could also occur in patients with certain other medical conditions or even, as in this case, in someone who'd previously undergone general anaesthesia with no problems.

And it was fatal if not correctly treated in time.

'*Has* to be,' she repeated. 'But I'm in the middle of the procedure. I can't close up yet.'

'I'll start to reverse the anaesthesia, and you'll have time before he comes out of it fully. Just make it quick. I'll hyperventilate him.'

'What's the dose?' Pat demanded. 'I—I've never dealt with this before.'

She had a container rattling with vials. An adult male patient like this could need as much as thirty-six of them before the danger was past.

'One mil per kilo, by rapid infusion,' Candace said, not raising her eyes from the surgical field. 'But I've heard it's hard to mix.'

'I'm shaking it. That's what the instructions say. But it's not— OK, it's mixing, I think it's all right.'

'You can give ten per kilo cumulatively. Check that, because that's from memory, and if I'm wrong... Drain, Doreen.'

'Did you say drain?'

'*Yes!* Peter, your hand's in the way. I need the cautery again, Doreen. Here's the organ. Steve, are you treating the heart problem?'

'Fifteen mils per kilo over ten minutes,' he muttered. 'Yes, and I've reversed the anaesthesia so you're on a clock.'

'IV saline, surface cooling...' she coached. 'Guys, you do it. I'm not talking you through it. I've got my own problems here.'

Like another bleed, and the blood was still looking too dark, showing its lack of oxygen. She needed the cautery again. Should she have picked up on this sooner? In hindsight, that blood had been darker than usual for a while.

While I was thinking about swimming with Steve in the sea pool...

'Temp's not coming down.'

'What is it?'

'Forty-one point six. His body is rigid.'

'Urine's discoloured,' Doreen said.

'I'm closing now,' Candace could report. She'd worked fast. Too fast, probably. She would be keeping an extra close eye on this patient's recovery over the next few days.

'Good. He's lightening, but he's not out,' Steve said.

'Good,' she echoed.

'OK, and we need sodium bicarbonate, IV glucose. Look at those levels!'

It took them another hour to bring Eric Kellett safely out of the crisis, and they all felt shaky, lucky and light-headed with relief when his temperature dropped, his heart rhythm stabilised and his other signs had begun to return to normal.

He was out in Recovery now, still hooked up to monitors and under close observation. He was on two different drugs for maintenance of urine output. His electrolytes, blood gases, central venous pressure and arterial pressure all needed to be carefully watched and adjusted as necessary, as did his potassium level.

The surgical team was back in Theatre, preparing for the next—delayed—procedure in an atmosphere that was still frayed and tensed.

'We nearly lost him. We damn near lost him,' Steve repeated.

'Stop saying that!' Candace snapped. But she was more angry at herself than at him. 'Have you ever had this happen in surgery before?'

'No,' he shook his head. 'I learned about it during my anaesthesia training but, you know, you tend to get complacent, lulled by the routine.'

'We throw away several dozen vials of this expensive drug every time it gets to its use-by date,' Pat confirmed. 'We never use it. We have it on hand, but in fifteen years here I've never had to use it. When I couldn't get it to mix, I got really scared there for a moment.' She shook her head, reliving the feeling.

'The trouble with a country hospital like this one is that anyone who's likely to have complications during surgery gets shipped out to Canberra or Sydney. And anyway, there were no indicators with this patient. I— No!' Steve shook his head again. 'Those are excuses. I should have been on top of it.'

'We *were* on top of it,' Peter Moody argued. 'We got him out of it.'

'*I* should have been onto it sooner!' Candace retorted. 'I've handled risky patients. People with Duchenne muscular dystrophy or osteogenesis imperfecta. I've done a lot more surgery than you, Steve. Than any of you. And I've seen malignant hyperthermia before. Admittedly, only once, as a resident, but I should have taken that rise in temperature more seriously as soon as you reported it.'

'There were no other symptoms at that stage,' Steve argued.

'There were. His blood was darker than usual. It should have clicked. But we should let it rest now. Let go of it. You're right, Peter, we did get him out of it. Thanks, everyone.' She took a deep breath. 'Who do we have next?'

'Look at the list. Whoever it is, they've had to wait a while!' Pat said.

Candace had to think hard before it came. Was on the point of doing as Pat had suggested and going to look at the list taped to the wall just outside Theatre, then remembered, 'That's right. Gwen Jolimont for a haemorrhoidectomy and vein-stripping. What's her status?'

'She's not down here yet.'

'She was a while ago, but they took her back up,' Doreen offered. 'They were wondering if you'd cancel.'

'I'll phone through to the ward and check for you if they know to bring her down again,' Sister Wallace said, appearing in the open doorway.

'Thanks, Robyn,' Candace said.

Slowly, the atmosphere returned to normal—on the surface at least. But there remained an element of tension which hadn't been there before. No one chatted this time. People jumped to attention every time Candace spoke. She excised the haemorrhoidal tissue and took out the tired veins with such a determination to stay focused that she actually wasn't particularly focused at all.

She'd temporarily lost her easy sense of control and cool-headedness, and realised only once the patient had been wheeled out to Recovery that she'd forgotten to give her a local. How could she have done that? It meant that Mrs Jolimont would be in a lot of pain when she woke up.

Which meant Steve and Robyn had to spend the next hour walking a tightrope with medication and monitors, because Mrs Jolimont's blood pressure was low—just 75/48 at one point—and that meant they couldn't afford to give her an adequate dose of the narcotic pain relief that she needed. Narcotics lowered blood pressure still further.

'The last patient on the list, the vasectomy, Gordon Southwell, has cancelled,' Pat reported. 'He and his wife had second thoughts.'

The news came as a relief.

As she headed for the shower, Candace heard Gwen Jolimont retching into a kidney dish.

'We'll give you something to stop it,' Sister Wallace soothed. 'I'm sorry you're having such a rotten time.'

And eventually the patient's blood pressure began to climb. In the tearoom, Steve was able to report to Candace, 'I'm increasing her pain relief now.'

'I should have given her that local. I *should* have picked up on that dark blood, Steve!'

Blindly, she gripped his forearm and felt its strength at once, as well as the ticklish, silky texture of the mist of dark hair that grew there.

'Steady on,' he said quietly, his head close to hers. 'Why the self-accusation? Those were my monitors. I should have been interpreting the data better, not just reporting it back to you. I mean, hell, we could *all* talk about what we should have done. Pat was panicking, Peter just stood back at first. The fact is, the patient didn't have any history to suggest an increased susceptibility to what is, as we've agreed, a very rare condition. He'd been under general anaesthesia before with no problem. We handled it, and he survived.'

'Too close for comfort.'

'Agreed. But let's put it behind us. Let go of it. You were the one who said it, before Gwen's surgery.'

'Yes, and then I forgot to give her a local because I hadn't put it behind me at all!'

'Let it go!'

Watching her face, Steve saw her tight little nod, and felt the way she was still clinging to his arm. Her touch stoked a glowing fire of satisfaction inside him and he twisted his hand to let his fingers trail along the sensitive skin of her inner arm. Her quick indrawn breath told him once more what he had been sure of all along. So did the way she unconsciously leaned closer, the way her limbs seemed to soften.

It wasn't finished. Whatever she had said to him ten days ago about her ex-husband, whatever the effect of his own angry words, it wasn't finished between them. He'd known it all along, and suddenly he wasn't prepared to bide his time any longer. She must know it, too. She *did* know it, just as he'd meant her to. They had both been holding their breath, waiting for the right moment, and it had come.

'I'll come round at about six,' he told her quietly and confidently. 'Let's go out. There's a nice seafood place on the riverfront. We can talk.'

'About what?'

'Whatever you like.'

He hadn't given her a choice, but he knew Candace wasn't the kind of woman to respond to an order if she didn't want to. Would she choose to be waiting for him tonight? Watching the dark dilation of her pupils and feeling the slight flutter and jerk of her breathing, he felt quite sure that she would be.

Candace *was* waiting.

Well, she wasn't going to absent herself from her own home just because of his threatened arrival! She hadn't changed her clothes, and still wore the loose ecru trousers and matching blouse in a linen-look fabric which she'd changed into after surgery. She was prepared to talk, and that was all. They could talk just as easily here as they could, dressed up to the nines, at an expensive restaurant. *More* easily, in fact.

Steve, however, was dressed for dinner. She hadn't seen him look this sophisticated before, hadn't known that he would carry the more formal look with such relaxed grace. Her reaction to him at her door disturbed her, and she knew that this was going to be harder than she'd been prepared for.

He wore a simple white T-shirt that closely hugged the contours of his chest and a blue-grey suit whose baggy jacket and pants created an impression of deceptive ease in the way he held his body.

'Come in,' she said. 'Tea, or—?'

'Tea?' he snorted. 'You can do better than that, Candace.'

'Better…in what way?'

'A better job of telling me to get lost. If you want me to get lost, show me the door. Don't make some insipid offer of tea that you hope will put me off. Come on, you're braver than that!'

'Am I?'

'Brave enough to make love to me on an open beach. Brave enough to tell me afterwards exactly what was going on…or what you thought was going on…inside your soul when it happened.'

'We've been through this.'

She closed her eyes, felt him closing in on her and opened them again quickly. She walked towards the kitchen in search of iced water or juice. Glasses in their hands would offer at least some faint form of protection.

'I've told you,' she said with her back to him, 'that was all about—'

'It *wasn't* all about Todd!' he cut in angrily, following her. 'I told you that at the time. I've been thinking about it since, and it doesn't make sense. Nothing in the way we made love, the way we responded to each other's bodies so strongly, that night and the other nights, was about proving something to your ex-husband, Candace, and after ten days of cooling off, you can admit it, I think!'

'Admit it to you?'

'Admit it to yourself. You wanted us to become lovers. Every cell in your body wanted it. And you got your wish, and then you back-pedalled as fast as you could. Because you were scared. Not because you were using me. Not because you were proving something. Isn't that the truth?'

Candace was silent.

The truth. She'd told Steve what she'd believed to be the truth ten days ago—that she'd been proving a foolish point to Todd, which her ex-husband would never even know about, and that she'd been coolly using Steve to do it.

Having said that, and having heard Steve's response, watched him leave her life—or leave her *personal* life, anyway—without more than a token protest, she'd expected the whole thing to subside into a feeling of uncomfortable regret. Perhaps even revulsion.

She'd been on the receiving end of confidences from single female friends more than once. She knew the pattern. 'We slept together twice,' they would say in an agony of regret, 'and now I can't understand what I ever saw in him. Why didn't I stop and think before I leapt into bed? There's no spark at all.'

But she didn't feel anything like that about Steve. Instead, she was all too aware of how easy it would be to let him back into her life, and into her bed.

And he knew it.

She was still fiddling at the sink, trying to get ice cubes out of the tray from the freezer, when he came up behind her, slid his arms around her, just beneath her breasts, and touched his lips to her neck.

'I like it when you have your hair pleated up like this,' he said. 'Makes it much easier to kiss you here. And then, later on, it's so nice to pull down...'

This was the moment to say no, to pull away, to show him the door, but she didn't do it. Instead, she gave a ragged sigh, turned around, leaned against him and waited for the onslaught of his mouth.

'You knew this would happen,' she murmured. 'You knew it...'

'Didn't you?' His lips were soft and slow, and his question was more kiss than language.

'No. I thought... I'd planned to... I tried to...' The words trailed off as her head fell back, her mouth drowning beneath his. 'Yes,' she admitted finally, pressing her forehead against his. 'I knew it.'

He kissed her again, then dragged his lips away and laughed. 'I wonder if you know how great it is that you can't resist this. The sight of you melting, of the same fire building in you that's building in me... It's so good to watch, Candace. So good.'

'Stop talking. Don't make me think too much...'

They didn't get to the restaurant until eight o'clock, and didn't leave it until it closed. He stayed all night at her place, and once again they both had to tackle appointment hours on empty stomachs. On the weekend, he took her swimming in the sea pool and for a hike in the bush, and as the days went by they added more activities to the repertoire.

'It all comes under the definition of things we do to fill in time until it's decently permissible to take each other off to bed again,' Steve teased.

She sighed, then smiled. 'Can't argue, can I?'

They talked on the phone about patients a little more than was strictly necessary. Eric Kellett had had no subsequent after-shocks of malignant hyperthermia and was recovering well from his surgery. As planned, Candace was particularly careful to check the site of his operation, but no complications developed. Steve had taken out Andrea Johnson's stitches in his surgery. Gwen Jolimont was pleased with the results of her two concurrent procedures after her difficult few hours in Recovery.

They ate take-out meals and watched movies, walked along the beach at night, watching the waves. Talked about trivial things, and important things. Brought a blanket to the beach at night sometimes, made love in the secret darkness and were careful about where they left their clothes.

They were careful about other things, too.

Firstly, contraception. Only once had this particular caution broken down—the first night they'd found their special hollow in the dunes.

Candace received her body's evidence that there were no unintended consequences to that piece of carelessness and electric spontaneity, but she hadn't been particularly worried in any case, as the timing had been wrong.

They were, if anything, even more careful about keeping their affair a secret from any of the staff at the hospital. Candace's focus and economy with conversation in surgery camouflaged their almost unnatural distance when they met at the hospital. The fact that Steve lived just five doors away made concealment easier, too. And there was a reason why they took most of their walks under the cover of darkness.

No one made any comments which suggested they'd guessed. And there was an element of luck as well. This was a small community. There were times they could have run into someone they knew on a hiking trail or in a restaurant. But they were lucky, and they didn't.

About four weeks after the night when they'd resumed their affair—the day of Eric Kellett's surgery—Candace received the first inkling that their caution in one of those two crucial areas hadn't been enough.

Her period was over a week late. Her breasts were swollen and tender. The smell of tomato ketchup made her nauseous, as did the smells of her bathroom cleaner, her moisturiser, the fuel she put in her car and about a dozen other everyday things.

It was impossible, surely. Steve had been very responsible in that area.

I'm imagining this, she decided. I have to be.

But those dates weren't her imagination, and all at once her memory of how she'd felt for the first few months of carrying Maddy, nearly sixteen years ago, was strikingly vivid.

She spent two more days talking herself out of it, refreshing her memory as to the statistical reliability of Steve's protection and coming up with as many rationalisations as she could. She had sensible theories like the fact that this was a new environment, and that she was still emerging from the emotional upheaval of the past couple of years. She also had ridiculous theories like the difference in the drinking water and the phases of the moon.

That was why her period was late. That was why she was feeling so queasy. It wasn't the obvious reason at all.

Yeah, right...

Finally, one Sunday morning, she drove an hour and a half north on the highway to a town with a pharmacy which had extended hours. She wanted one where there was no danger of being recognised at the counter as she paid for a pregnancy testing kit.

I won't do the test until I get home, she decided.

Ten minutes later, she screeched to a halt beside a small park, locked herself into one of the cubicles in the surprisingly clean and airy public toilet and began to fiddle about with the plastic testing wand. The result only took a minute or two to appear in the little window.

And there was no doubt. It was positive.

'Hey, nice surprise,' Steve said when he found Candace at his door just after lunch. 'I was heading for the beach. Want to come?'

'Um, no.'

'No?'

He stopped in the act of slinging his towel around his neck. The surf was dead flat today, so he wasn't bothering with wetsuit or board. Looked like he might not even be getting a swim.

Studying her face more closely, he noted her high colour, her distracted manner and the firm press of her lips. Felt a little prickle of apprehension. She wasn't going to have another try at ending this, was she? He felt selfish about it.

Don't rock the boat, he wanted to say. Don't keep analysing it and asking questions. You said you wanted an affair. And it's working as it is, isn't it?

Better than 'working'. Lord, he was loving his discovery of this woman!

He loved the vein of wickedness in her newly unleashed sensuality. A couple of weeks ago, she'd eaten a dessert of fresh raspberries and whipped cream off his chest, making the action of her tongue deliberately erotic until they'd both collapsed in laughter.

He loved the way she worked with such efficiency and focus, loved the things that tickled her sense of humour, loved the impression she sometimes unconsciously gave that she was shedding an old, painful skin now that she was here in Australia, and that she was ready to tackle life in new ways.

He was aware, though, of just how new their connection was. Less than two months. Intuition and chemistry aside, human beings were complex, and there were a lot of things he didn't know about her yet. Had they spent too much time in bed? There was still a strong possibility that this affair could drift into very dangerous waters…

'Uh…Steve, we have something to discuss,' she began.

'*Again?*' The word slipped out before he thought, and he saw her flinch.

'No, this is something new,' she said steadily, then gave a short laugh. '*Extremely* new.'

'Along the same lines of ''new'' as the raspberries and cream, I hope.'

'Don't.' She took a deep breath. 'Lord, I just have to *say* it, don't I? Steve, I'm pregnant.'

Whump!

That was the sound of his backside hitting the couch with force. He suddenly knew what the expression 'legs turned to jelly' meant, in a way he never had before. Beyond the beating of blood in his head, he had wit enough to understand at once that his first reaction to this news was critical. Still, the only thing he could come up with at first was, 'That's…a surprise.'

'I know.' She nodded. 'I mean, it isn't really. It happens. We've, um, been doing our best. But, yes, it's a surprise.' She flushed, then smiled, and that gave him his first clue.

She's thrilled.

He took a deep breath. The frog in his throat doubled in size. 'Congratulations,' he managed, and she beamed.

Then she frowned, pressed her palms to her cheeks and gabbled, 'It's crazy to be happy about it. But I am. I'm sorry, it's— I'm just telling you. I'm not asking for anything. Haven't worked out…well, *anything*. Not yet.'

'What does it mean for us?' he said, suspecting it was probably one of the questions she wanted to ask him herself.

She spread her hands, just as Steve might have done. 'Don't know.'

'I'm not going to turn my back on you,' he promised.

It was vague, he felt, but sincere. God, what *did* you promise? Nothing that might turn out, later, to be unfair. Nothing that she might interpret wrongly, or magnify too much. As he'd thought before, in a slightly different context, he wasn't yet fully certain of the job description here.

'I didn't think you would,' she said.

There was a light shining in her eyes. It panicked him considerably.

'But I'm not going to marry you either,' he said, too abruptly. 'Not out of the blue. It wouldn't be fair. Or sensible.'

Her chin came up. 'I'm not asking you to marry me, Steve. I hadn't expected this sort of a connection between us either. I'm here for a year. This was—'

'A fling, right?' The word didn't taste right. It reminded him of Agnetha, and he didn't like it. He'd stopped comparing Candace with Agnetha a long time ago. 'I mean—'

'No, it's a good word,' she said. 'Let's not... Let's keep this honest. That's been working for us, hasn't it?'

'Yeah, it has.'

'This is going to take some working out.'

'And yet you're thrilled,' he pointed out softly. 'Don't try and deny it, because it's shining like a hundred-watt globe in your face, Candace. Why are you thrilled?'

She laughed. 'Because...'

Then she burst into tears.

His instinct was to go to her, and he did. Privately, though, his panic level was climbing. Just how much of this sort of thing were they both in for? They'd known each other for less than two months They didn't have the foundation for this. Mood swings and nausea, weight gain, aching legs...and *gossip*, for heaven's sake, because eventually people would have to know...

And at the end of all that, a baby. A human being, made from the two of them. Candace's due date would come just a month or two before she was due to return home. Unless she cut short her time here and went back to Boston early. Would he want that? He didn't know.

Oh, yes, and he was panicked all right. He gritted his teeth and willed it not to show, held her, chafed her back lightly with his palms and waited. She controlled herself quickly and apologised. 'Oops! Where did that come from?'

'It's fine,' he said.

'Ah, no, you were terrified.' She smiled, slid out of his arms, wagged a finger at him, grabbed a tissue from the end table and dried her eyes and nose. 'Nine months of hormones ahead. Who wouldn't be terrified?'

'Well...'

'Look, it's simple.'

'Tell me, then.' He tried not to make it sound too desperate. 'I need to hear something simple.'

'I loved having Maddy,' she said. 'I always wanted another baby. My ex-husband convinced me we shouldn't. Now I'm having one, and against all logic—I'm very capable of *rec-*

ognizing logical behaviour, Steve, even if I can't produce it right now—I'm thrilled. I'm going to live inside that feeling for a little while, then start making sensible plans when the dust has settled.'

When will that be? he wondered inwardly. I've got dust to settle, too.

'Wanted to tell you straight away,' she went on, 'because—well, because I believe it's your right to know.'

His right to know.

Just that? Or could he claim more than that?

His right to be involved.

At the moment, he sensed, neither of them knew.

CHAPTER SIX

'I CAN'T stand it, Mom. Can you talk to Dad and ask if I can stay with Grammy until school's out? Then I'm going to come and have summer vacation with you,' Maddy announced on the phone, on a Monday morning near the end of May, without pausing for breath.

Candace, in contrast, had to pause for quite a large, long, careful breath before she replied. Almost eight and a half weeks pregnant now, she was feeling very queasy for much of the time.

'Till school's out,' she repeated. 'That's, what, about two weeks from now?'

'Tell Dad you're missing me.'

'It's true. I'm missing you a lot. I knew I would.'

'And you want me there. Tell him to get me a ticket. Brittany's driving me nuts, and the baby cries all the time.'

'I expect that drives *her* nuts.'

'He's adorable when he's not crying. Like, the three minutes per day when he's not crying! She has this pile of baby-care books about six feet high beside her bed, and it's all she ever talks about. How to get him to not cry. I try not to be home. I practically live at Alicia's or Grammy's. In fact, if I could live at Grammy's until you get back next March, it just *might* stop me from going totally insane. I think Brittany's over-feeding him.'

'How would you know that, honey?'

'He's getting fat! She gives him, like, twelve bottles a day. And *that* I know because for some reason it's my job to wash and sterilise them. Figure that out! Suddenly, it's tied to my allowance. Which, admittedly, has been doubled,' she drawled, and Candace had to laugh.

She wanted to say, I love you, but knew the reception these words would receive. Instead, she kept listening.

'And we never eat properly. Dad picks up take-out practically every night. You know, I wouldn't have thought I could get sick of junk food but I'm here to tell you, it's happened. You should be so pleased with me! I want salad, and that casserole you make...'

'OK, enough! I'd love it if you came out.' Which was close to I love you but not quite as bad.

'Then Grammy will come a couple of weeks later, and we'll go home together, because I have to be back for drama camp,' Maddy said happily, betraying the fact that the thing was a done deal before she even picked up the phone.

Both of them! Candace thought. An attack on two fronts. And Elaine and Maddy had always been as thick as thieves.

Her stomach dropped.

'So when exactly will that be, honey?'

'About the end of July. Grammy can only take two weeks.'

I'll be nearly four months pregnant by then, and if this one's the same as Maddy, I'll already be starting to show, to anyone who takes a close look. Mom might easily guess. And a few weeks after that, everyone will.

Candace hadn't faced this inevitable development yet. Hadn't faced a lot of things. Was concentrating, to a large extent, on simply getting through the days without her condition becoming obvious to her colleagues immediately. She felt horribly ill, especially if she ate the wrong foods at the wrong times or if she didn't get enough rest—and that meant at least ten hours' sleep out of every twenty-four.

Her slower work pace, here in Australia, was the only thing that made it possible to keep her pregnancy a secret. She slept late whenever she could, went to bed early, took a nap in the middle of the day at least twice a week, and lived on a steady intake of finger foods like crackers and grapes and toast.

Being pregnant at almost thirty-nine was very different to being pregnant at twenty-two, she found.

It wasn't just her increased fatigue and nausea. There was also the question of prenatal testing. It hadn't been an issue with Maddy. Back then, she'd had every expectation of giving birth to a healthy baby, and she hadn't been disappointed. This time, a decision had to be made, and it was one of many things that she and Steve hadn't talked about.

They were still seeing each other. Nothing had yet given them a reason to end their affair. This had to count as a plus. It was like walking on eggshells, most of the time, however. Not wanting to drag him down, Candace did her best to pretend, when they were together, that she wasn't pregnant at all. She got a lot of practice at this during surgery and office hours, so she was getting rather good at it.

Steve, on the other hand, treated her as if she were made of tissue paper. He probably wouldn't have made love to her at all if she hadn't seduced him every time. When she did, he left her in no doubt that he appreciated the effort, and this began to form a nourishing centre to their fresh young relationship.

Her body was exquisitely sensitive to his touch at the moment, and he was so determined to be gentle that time seemed to stretch and hours would go by...

It couldn't continue this way. They needed to do more than just laze about together.

'I'm starting to know this look,' Steve said to her, greeting her at his front door on the evening of the day that Maddy had called. He tilted his head a little as he studied her. 'Come in, all three of you.'

'All three?'

She frowned as she eased past him into the welcoming, warmly lit interior of his living room. She liked his place. It was relaxed yet cosy, decorated in a simpler and more masculine version of her own rented house nearby. The blues he'd used were a little darker, like the ocean in a storm, and they were offset by cool cream instead of sunny yellow. She was beginning to feel at home here. Too much so, maybe.

'Yes,' he answered her. 'All three. You, the baby and that packet of chips you're hugging. It's almost as big as you are.'

'I was hungry, and I knew if I didn't—'

'Bring the chips and start munching on them at once, you'd throw up. I know. Here, let me help,' he said, taking the packet from its cradled position in her arms and ripping it apart at the top.

He handed the opened packet back to her, then touched her face gently and slid his fingers back over her loosened hair. 'Have you come for dinner?' he asked.

'I've started on dinner already,' she said, crunching down on a huge curvy chip. The salt was heaven, and her stomach lay down obediently. It was a pity that the effect wouldn't last.

'I haven't,' he said. 'Started cooking, that is. So what do you feel like?'

'Nothing.'

'Pasta?'

'Fine. But it can wait.'

He took her in his arms and rocked her to and fro, shifting his weight easily from side to side. 'Poor thing. Sit down, eat your chips, and tell me about that look.'

'The…?'

'The look on your face. A number three, if I'm reading it right. It's the one that says we've got something to talk about.'

'Right. Gosh! You've got a numbering system for my expressions!'

'Sit!'

Gently, he pushed her down onto the couch and sat beside her. There was something immensely comforting about the warm press of his thigh along hers.

Or perhaps it was the chips.

Taking another one, she leaned her head into his shoulder, felt his arm drop around her and decided, no, it isn't either of those things. It's the fact that he can read my expressions. It's nice.

Aloud, she said, 'We need to make a decision about prenatal testing, Steve. A chorionic biopsy is ideally done at about eleven weeks, and I'm already eight and a half.'

'I know,' he said quietly. 'I was going to give you three more days and then bring up the subject myself.'

'Why three more days? You didn't need to wait. You could have brought it up whenever you wanted. Has it been on your mind?'

'On my mind? What do you think?' His voice rose abruptly, and he slid away from her, sprang to his feet and began to pace the room. 'Of course it has, after what happened to Matt and Helen! Good grief, Candace!'

She gasped and stumbled instinctively to stand as well, then had to stop and clutch her stomach, gripped by nausea.

'Oh, hell, I'm sorry,' she muttered through clenched teeth. Her lips were tight and dry, and the nausea was threatening to take over completely. It was an effort to look across at him. 'I'm so sorry. I didn't even think about that...'

This was one of the problems with a secret affair. She hadn't actually met Steve's brother and his wife. It was more than two months since Matt and Helen had lost their baby at birth, and Candace had been feeling so ill and exhausted these past few weeks, with such a struggle to pretend that everything was normal, she hadn't considered the way the issue must resonate for him.

It had been thoughtless of her. She was about to apologise again, but he got in first.

'No, I'm sorry. I shouldn't have yelled at you.'

'No, I want you to yell at me.' She gave a short, wry laugh. 'I deserved it. And I'm not that fragile. You can yell at me whenever you like.'

'Let's forget it. I know you've had…other things to think about. Tell me what you want to do about prenatal testing.'

He pulled an upright chair out from the table in the dining nook and sat in it with his legs straddling the seat and his forearm resting along the back. He studied her gravely, and some strands of his glinting mid-brown hair fell across his forehead.

'It's your decision, too.' She subsided to the couch again, still needing to move cautiously to keep her stomach under control.

He was silent, then said carefully, 'Not necessarily. Your home is in America, Candace. We can't ignore that. Realistically, this child isn't going to be nearly such a huge presence in my life as it is in yours, no matter what we decide about access and that sort of thing. We've made no commitment to each other. We've agreed on that. I can't force my feelings or my beliefs on you.'

'No,' she agreed. 'But I still want to know what they are.'

He nodded. 'Fair enough.' Then he spoke slowly. 'I guess...I'd feel on surer ground if we knew that there was nothing to worry about. The risk of having a Down's baby at your age is about one in 135. People bet on those odds all the time when it's something they want. A problem with the baby is something we don't want.'

Candace nodded, then thought for a minute, aware of him watching her. His strong chin dug into his forearm and his eyes were narrowed and serious. For a man who had such a deep vein of physicality to his make-up—a man who was such an ideal candidate for a fling—Steve Colton had a considerable depth of intellect and sensitivity as well, she was starting to realise.

'If Helen and Matt had had the test done,' she said finally, carefully, 'what would their decision have been?'

'I don't know,' he answered simply. 'I don't know what my decision would be either. Maybe it'd have to happen, I'd have to be *told*, yes, the test has come back showing that the baby has Down's—or one of the other trisomies, which are less likely but can be even more severe in their effects—before I could be certain of what I'd want to do.'

She sat up higher and looked at him. 'Have you been reading my mind or something?'

'Yes, I get a bulletin over the internet every morning,' he teased. 'No, why?'

'I—I think that's what I was going to say, only I hadn't managed to even work it out yet. I want the test, Steve, even if it's only in order to know more about what lies ahead.'

Without a word, he came to the couch, sat beside her and pulled her close. He pressed his forehead against hers, and they sat like that for several minutes. Finally, he kissed her. It was sweet and slow, tender but without erotic demand. Just the kiss she needed.

'Come and help me make pasta,' he said finally. 'What sort of sauce do you feel like?'

'From a jar?'

'Doesn't have to be. I'm very flexible. What do you *feel* like?' he asked again.

She closed her eyes to think, trying hard to get enthusiastic about food in any form. 'Um, something simple and salty. No tomato. No meat. Or I think I'd—'

'I know what you'd do, Candee.'

'Sorry.' She crunched quickly on another chip.

'Leave it to me. I'll invent something with a heavy emphasis on salt.'

It was on the table in fifteen minutes, just a tangle of fettucini coated in bits of olive and garlic, anchovy, fresh parsley and cheese. She would have enjoyed it immensely if anything at all had tasted right at the moment.

'So I've been thinking,' he said as they ate. 'We should go to Sydney for the test.'

'That far?'

'Not very many people choose a chorionic biopsy around here. People don't have testing done at all, or they go for amniocentesis, which is done at around fifteen weeks.'

'I don't want to wait that long.'

'I agree. But if you go with CVS, you need an obstetrician who's experienced with the procedure, and that means Sydney or Canberra. There's the added bonus of privacy,' he went on, after a short pause.

She didn't argue the point. She did consider protesting his assumption that secrecy remained so important. They'd agreed on that two and a half months ago, but maybe it was time this changed.

No. Not yet. Secrecy *was* important still, she revised after a few moments' thought.

She didn't want the pressure of colleagues or friends or, heaven help her, Mom or Maddy asking about their plans. The future stretched a little further ahead in her mind now than it had done an hour ago. It went as far as the chorionic biopsy and the result, which would come around three weeks later once the tissue from the placenta had been cultured.

Beyond that, her life was a fog.

'We can finesse this a bit,' Steve was saying. 'I can write you the referral letter myself. I'd go with Ian Strickland in Sydney. He's very good. We'll make it a Friday, if possible, and stay overnight. Maybe the whole weekend.'

'You keep saying *we*,' she accused lightly.

'Yes.' He looked at her, his blue gaze very direct across the table. 'Of course I'm saying *we*. You don't think I'd let you go through it alone, do you?'

She could have cried at that point. Managed not to.

'Maddy's coming,' she blurted suddenly instead. 'My daughter.'

Why had she added those last words? Of course he knew who Maddy was!

'When?'

'In two or three weeks. She called this morning to see if it was OK, but really she'd already made up her mind, with my mother to back her up. They're natural allies, those two.'

'And *is* it OK?'

'Yes, it's great.' She laughed, and added, 'It's wonderful, and I haven't got the remotest idea how I'm going to handle it.'

'The very first thing you should do is phone her and make sure she doesn't plan an itinerary that clashes with the optimum timing of the test,' he said. 'As to the rest, worry about it later.'

'I'm getting good at worrying about things later. Better than I want to be.' She looked down at her half-eaten plate of pasta, and this time the fight against tears was harder to win.

The landscape on the Saturday morning drive up to Sydney hadn't changed much in three months.

Although it was early winter now, native Australian trees didn't lose their leaves, and the weather wasn't cold enough to make the grass turn brown. If anything, the late autumn rains had made the landscape greener than before. The sky was still blue, and there was even some vegetation that was still in flower.

Curled in the passenger seat of Steve's car with a pillow behind one shoulder and a mohair blanket over her knees, Candace felt dreamy and content as the pretty vistas unfolded. She was exactly at the eleven-week mark now, had begun to feel—cautiously—a little less nauseous, and was looking forward to this weekend away.

Steve had booked the two of them into a bed-and-breakfast place at Cremorne Point on Sydney Harbour's northern shore, and tonight they were going to dinner near the Opera House, followed by a big, splashy musical. Tomorrow they would explore the Harbour and the city, on Monday she was scheduled for the chorionic biopsy with Dr Strickland, and on Tuesday morning Maddy would arrive.

'Dropping off to sleep?' Steve asked as they swept around a wide curve of highway and saw the ocean and a string of coastal settlements in the distance.

'Not really,' she said. 'Sleepy, but the view is too pretty to waste it by closing my eyes.'

'Nice for some,' he teased. 'I have to watch the road.'

'We can swap. You've trusted me at the wheel of your car before.'

'We're not swapping.'

He was still treating her like a fragile porcelain figurine, and since this was how she felt most of the time, she found it easy to give in to it and let him do it.

Maybe that's why I don't want to sleep, she decided. This weekend might be precious—a precious memory—and I don't want to lose any of it...

An hour later, they stopped at a beachside park in one of Sydney's southern suburbs on Botany Bay. Steve had packed a picnic lunch of thick, chewy ham and salad sandwiches on French bread, as well as tea and some buttered buns with lurid frosting of a very thick and sticky pink.

'No, thanks!' Candace said with a shudder, when he offered her one.

'May I have yours, too, then?'

'Honestly, I've tasted these! If you said you needed them as a substitute for rubber cement, maybe, but to *eat*? *Two* of them?'

He grinned. 'Can't call yourself an Australian if you don't like a nice wad of sticky bun on occasion.'

'I *don't* call myself an Australian,' she pointed out.

He shrugged. 'True.'

A huge Qantas 747 jet lumbered down the airport runway, which jutted into Botany Bay less than two kilometres from where they sat at a picnic bench beneath bright green Norfolk pines. It gathered speed, engines screaming, and finally heaved itself off the ground, to rise steeply over the shallow water of the bay and wheel to the north-west, heading across the Pacific.

Where was it going? Home, maybe. To America, where Maddy's bedroom in Boston was probably a mess of half-packed suitcases right at this moment.

This time in two days, she'll be on the plane. This time in three days, she'll be here...

'You can't wait, can you?' Steve said. He had followed her yearning gaze as she tracked the plane.

'Reading my mind again?' she retorted.

'Reading your face.'

'What number look is this?'

'Number two,' he answered in the blink of an eye. 'You think about her a lot, don't you?'

'Of course!'

'Why didn't you bring her with you?'

Because she would have drastically inter-fered with the launch of my fling with you.

Something told her very firmly not to follow this thought any further. It led into a wilderness of conjecture that was pointless to explore.

'Maddy wanted to stay at home,' she said instead. 'Australia was a place in a movie, as far as she was concerned. Snakes and sharks, little wooden shacks in the middle of a treeless desert and men in crocodile-skin hats.'

'Great!' He laughed. 'Remind me to hunt up my crocodile skin hat as soon as we get back.'

'It wasn't a place to hang out with friends and start dating cute boys and get elected class president. I didn't push it. I *wanted* to. But it wouldn't have been fair. And she's always been pretty independent. Going off to summer camp without a backward glance from when she was eight. Even when she says she's missing me, she's somehow speaking from a position of strength. No, this was…something I needed for me. Getting away like this. For her, too, I guess. I'll be a better mother when I get back.' A self-mocking laugh escaped her lips. 'Not so bitter and twisted—'

She stopped abruptly.

A *better* mother? A completely different mother. A single mother with a newborn baby. It didn't seem real. She couldn't picture it at all. So much so that she'd actually forgotten for a moment, while talking about Maddy, that she was pregnant. With this man's child.

Steve was watching her, his body lazy, his mouth a little crooked and his eyes hard to read.

'OK, what number look is this?' she challenged him, unnerved by his body language and by the movement of her own thoughts.

'Don't know,' he answered casually. 'Haven't seen this one before. Ready to get going?'

'Yes, because I think, actually, when we get to our bed-and-breakfast, I'll take a nap.'

Suddenly she felt exhausted, and she'd had enough of the planes. The sight of them taking off and landing was dramatic and beautiful in this setting, but these big jumbo jets were a constant reminder that the world was a big place. Too big for a woman who was carrying a child with a heritage split in two by the vastness of the Pacific Ocean.

She wasn't sorry when they drove off, went through a tunnel on the highway that actually ran beneath the airport runway and left the planes behind.

*   *   *

Their harbourside bed-and-breakfast turned out to be delightful. Antique furnishings, complimentary drinks and snacks, fluffy towels, fragrant linens and gorgeous water views.

'It'll just be a little nap,' Candace promised when they'd unpacked.

'No worries. I'll go for a walk, explore the Point and watch the ferries going past.'

'Half an hour.'

But she slept for two, and only awoke when he slid into bed beside her, without clothes. 'Couldn't keep away any longer,' he muttered. 'Is that all right?'

'You know it is. It always is.'

'I've been watching you for ten minutes, and you looked so good...'

She turned into his arms and kissed his mouth softly, still unsettled about those planes and that vast ocean. She wanted to drug herself with his love-making and just forget everything else.

He obliged with delicious tenderness, then they showered together and his slippery, soapy hands on her body—'All my favourite places, your hips, your stomach, your breasts...they feel even better these days...you're beginning to ripen, Candace'—seemed to promise that nothing else mattered but this, and now, and the two of them.

They had dinner overlooking the Opera House and the ferry terminal at Circular Quay, then saw the show they had tickets for. It was light and sophisticated and very well done. The next morning, they breakfasted on a glassed-in terrace at their B and B, then caught the ferry across to Circular Quay and back out to Manly, passing huge cargo ships as well as a gleaming white cruise liner and dozens of colourful sailboats.

The ferry crossed the gap between the harbour heads, rocking more in the rougher water, and they caught glimpses of the spectacular houses that fronted the Harbour, as well as wilder sections of rock and vegetation on the northern shore. At Manly they ate Lebanese falafel rolls and ice cream for lunch.

In the afternoon, they explored the steps around the Opera House and the historic Rocks area, with its lingering flavour of the First Fleet's settlement over two hundred years earlier. That evening, they ate in Chinatown, then walked through Darling Harbour and caught a water taxi back to Cremorne Point. It zipped beneath the dark, awe-inspiring metal fretwork of the Harbour Bridge and skirted Kirribilli

Point, where the two historic residences of Admiralty House and Kirribilli House sat grandly amidst their lush gardens.

'It has to be the most beautiful harbour in the world,' Candace said, as they alighted from the water taxi at Cremorne Wharf and walked beneath huge Moreton Bay fig trees back to their B and B.

'Sydneysiders certainly think so,' Steve said.

'You think it has some competition?'

'Hong Kong is pretty nice. Vancouver. New York.'

'I didn't realise you'd travelled so much.'

'I like travelling. I'd like to get to the US again pretty soon.'

For a moment, with the mention of her native soil, they both teetered on the edge of pulling this casual conversation in a more important direction. Candace could feel it. She was holding her breath, waiting. The sense of expectancy, the sense that they were both thinking about it, trying to find the right questions, the right words, was almost unbearable.

But then they reached the front door of the B and B, which was locked at this time of night. They couldn't remember which of them had the key, and the moment passed.

*   *   *

At ten the next morning, Candace had her chorionic biopsy at Royal North Shore Hospital.

She hadn't spent much time thinking about the process of the test itself. Obstetrics wasn't her area, and she vaguely thought that it involved going through the opening of the cervix in order to extract a tissue sample from the foetal side of the placenta. She did know that it would be done with the aid of an ultrasound scan, and had to drink and hold an agonising amount of fluid in order to create a clear image. The ultrasound waves bounced better off a full bladder.

Fortunately, Dr Strickland was on time and she was soon lying on the table in the darkened room, next to the sophisticated scanning equipment. The obstetrician ran through some information which both Candace and Steve already understood—that the test could detect any one of hundreds of chromosomal abnormalities, most of them extremely rare.

'Down's syndrome is the real concern,' Dr Strickland explained. 'And at your age...' he checked her notes briefly '...the risk of you miscarrying as a result of this procedure is approximately the same as your risk of carrying a Down's baby. Do you want to consider that risk a little further before you decide to go ahead with the test? Or consider what your decision would be if the test does reveal a problem?'

Candace looked instinctively at Steve. He reached out and took her hand, and she was suddenly flooded with warmth. However uncertain the future might be, with their shared agreement that no commitment to each other had been made, at least he was here with her now, and giving all she could have asked for.

'I think…' she began hesitantly, then was relieved when Steve took up her reply.

'I think we've talked about it enough beforehand,' he said. 'We're both doctors. We're aware of all the issues. But it was good to have it spelled out again.'

'We'll go ahead with the test,' Candace finished.

Dr Strickland's ultrasound technician spread a clear gel on her lower abdomen, established a picture on the black and white monitor and keyed in some details on the keyboard.

'There's the baby,' Dr Strickland murmured, as the technician slid the probe back and forth to find the best position. 'Alive and kicking. Literally!'

Steve and Candace were both silent.

Awed?

She was. Didn't know about Steve. She was watching the monitor intently, but felt the warm pressure of his hand as he gave her rather clammy fingers a squeeze.

The technician took some measurements, expertly manipulating the probe and using the keyboard to change the scale of the image or freeze it.

'The baby's size and development are both consistent with the dates you've given, Dr Fletcher,' Ian Strickland said, then added, 'Jenny, let's take a closer look at the spine, can we?'

There was a silence, broken only by the click of the keyboard and the hum of the machine. 'Freeze that, can you?' the obstetrician said. 'Yes, there.'

'What are we looking at?' Steve said, sounding a little edgy.

Candace was feeling that way, too, now. She'd expected to move more quickly to the biopsy itself, although it was magic to actually see the baby like this. In another couple of months, she'd be able to feel all that kicking and tumbling the tiny foetus was doing. When she'd thought for so many years that she'd never again take part in the miracle of creating a life, it was amazing.

'You said you were both doctors,' the obstetrician said. 'How familiar are you with this area of medicine?'

'Not very,' Steve answered for them both. 'I guess we know the theory.'

Candace's heart had started beating faster. Like Steve, she might not be an expert on foetal development and prenatal testing, but she was definitely an expert on the way specialists worded things to their patients when they weren't completely happy about what they saw.

'There's a problem, isn't there?' she demanded.

'Well, no, I wouldn't say that,' the specialist answered carefully.

'Something's not right. Something's ambiguous on the scan,' she insisted, then realised that her protest, in a rising voice tone, was only delaying his explanation. 'I'm sorry,' she said. 'Just tell us.'

'I'm looking at this measurement here,' he said, elbowing the technician aside politely and taking control of the keyboard and probe himself. 'The thickness of the skin in the neck area—the nuchal fold. Can you see it?'

'We can see it,' Steve came in quickly. 'What about it? Hell, there is something, isn't there?'

'Thickened skin in the nuchal fold, at this stage of development, can be an indicator of Down's,' came the blunt words.

Candace's whole body grew hot, then ice-cold. Yes. Yes, she'd known that, but she hadn't thought about it in a personal context.

Dear God!

Her thoughts were ragged, yet crystal clear.

I'll love you anyway... I'll keep you... I couldn't let you go...

'An indicator,' Steve echoed. 'I'm not thinking clearly. Can you go through the facts on it?'

'It's just that,' the obstetrician said. 'An indicator. There's a link. It's not definitive, by any means.'

He gave them some statistics which to Candace were, frankly, total gobbledygook right now. Then he said that if they were in any doubt about having the test, this information might cement their decision.

'We weren't in any doubt,' Steve said grimly. 'And we're not now. My brother and his wife had a Down's baby a few months ago and he died shortly after birth.'

'That's tragic for them,' Ian Strickland replied. 'But there's no correlation.'

'On paper,' Steve said. 'I know there isn't. Let me tell you, that feels completely meaningless at the moment! Emotionally, believe me, there's a correlation!'

'I can understand that,' the obstetrician said.

His manner was textbook perfect—controlled yet compassionate. Candace had spoken like that to patients herself when breaking difficult news. She suddenly realised, Lord, people must hate me sometimes! Must hate *all* of us, no matter how hard we try and how genuinely we care. It's in the nature of the job. I *loathe* this guy, and it's not his fault at all.

Candace cleared her throat with difficulty. 'So it's just a matter of having the test and waiting for the result,' she said. 'There's no short cut to getting a more concrete answer on this?'

Oh, for goodness' sake! I know there isn't! Darling baby, bouncing around on the screen, I don't want you to have Down's...

'I'm afraid not,' he answered. 'We'll all have to wait.'

'Can we get on with it, then, please?' Her voice was high.

She felt Steve's hand squeezing hers, harder this time. His was clammy now, too. As a ludicrously mundane counterpoint to the new question mark over the baby's condition, Candace's bladder felt as if it might soon explode.

The actual biopsy passed in a painful blur. Dr Strickland used a swab of numbing agent on the skin of her abdomen, and only then did she realise in some surprise, He's not going through the cervix after all. I'm out of date on that, or else they do it differently here.

Another time, she might have asked about it, but she didn't today.

Using the image on the screen as a guide, he then carefully inserted the hollow needle. She felt pressure and pain as it passed through the firm barrier of the abdominal muscles and the uterus, then a gentle release as it reached the placenta. The needle was visible on the screen as a fine line.

'Everything's very well positioned,' Dr Strickland said. 'The baby's well away from the needle.'

He drew back on the syringe, extracted the cells he needed and withdrew the needle. Placing the sample in a sterile specimen container, he held it up for Candace and Steve to see. It was pinkish-yellow in colour.

'That's a nice sample,' he said. 'We'll get an unequivocal result from it. Now, the main risk of miscarriage comes when we *don't* get a clean insertion of the needle and a good sample on the first try. If I'd hit the wrong spot and had to have a second or third attempt at it, I'd have been concerned. In this case, there was no problem, but you may still feel some cramping for the next twenty-four hours. Take it easy. Bed-rest would be ideal, and would give you more confidence, but it's not essential.'

'We planned on bed-rest,' Candace said.

'Take a few minutes here, too. You don't have to jump up. I don't need the room for a while.'

'Actually, I *do* need to jump up...'

He understood at once. 'Bathroom's just around the corner on the left.'

'Thanks.'

Steve was still sitting in the chair beside the patient's table in the ultrasound room when Candace returned. She entered the room on the tail end of the ultrasound technician, Jenny Sabatini, murmuring, 'Mmm...mmm,' to Steve and nodding sympathetically, with a frown tightly knitting her brows. She was a motherly type, and it sounded as if he'd been having a heart-to-heart with her.

I wonder what he said.

'Going to lie down again?' he asked her, taking her hand to give it a brief squeeze.

'Five minutes. My stomach does feel sore, and I felt the uterus cramp up a bit in the bathroom.'

She massaged the area around her navel. It was too soon to feel the baby there, but her abdomen felt different all the same. The webbing of muscle had started to loosen, ready for its imminent expansion. And there was psychology at work, too. She knew that the uterus had begun to grow, and that there was a fragile new life inside her. It very definitely felt different.

Steve helped her back onto the table and the ultrasound technician left, on a murmured, 'Good luck, both of you.'

'Want to lie on your side?' Steve asked.

'Yes, please.'

'There you go. Take as long as you like.'

He rested his hand on her shoulder, then rubbed it back and forth, the way he might have rubbed a child's bumped knee. Candace said nothing. She felt fragile and heavy and numb.

It wasn't real. They didn't *know* that there was a problem with the baby. It wasn't the same as Helen's and Matt's loss. But they knew that there *might* be—not just an abstract statistical possibility, but a concrete 'indication' in that thicker-than-usual skin at the back of the inch-long foetus's neck.

The news created a kind of grieving that was as real and difficult in its way as the grieving that Helen and Matt must still be dealing with. From the beginning, this pregnancy hadn't been simple, and now it was even less so.

I don't want you to have Down's, little baby...

There was still the faint possibility of miscarriage. There was the agonising wait for the result of the biopsy, and the knowledge of a potential decision to be made then—a painful, huge and life-changing decision which would vitally affect several lives.

In my heart, the decision's made already, but I'm not kidding myself that living with it would be easy...

There was Maddy's imminent arrival, followed in two and a half weeks by the arrival of Maddy's redoubtable grandmother.

With all this, Candace's relationship with Steve—that sizzling, superficial 'fling', which she'd entered into with such high hopes as to its therapeutic value—seemed like it had become lost in the shuffle.

Still lying on her side on the ultrasound table, she felt his arm slide along hers and the press of his chest against her upper back. His cheek brushed her face, still smooth from his shave this morning. It was only eleven o'clock.

'I'm sorry,' he whispered at last. 'I'm so sorry, Candace.'

And that was all.

CHAPTER SEVEN

MADDY got off the plane on schedule at ten to seven the next morning. Her eyelids were creased from lack of sleep, but she seemed energised and excited about being there, and she was a precious and beautiful sight to Candace.

Hugging her daughter tightly, she came out with the most hackneyed line in the world.

'You've grown.'

Maddy rolled her eyes beneath a mess of dark blonde hair and groaned. *'That's* all you can say?'

'For now. Give me time. I'm working on a big speech.' She turned to Maddy's heavily laden baggage cart. 'My lord, you've brought *three* suitcases? For four and a bit weeks?'

Maddy shrugged and grinned, impervious to the criticism. 'Couldn't decide, so I brought everything.'

She chattered about her luggage and the flight as they eased through the crowds towards the exit, and it was some moments before Candace managed to present Steve, who was doing a good job of hovering in the back-ground, despite his height and strong physical presence.

Candace was nervous about the introduc-tion, and wished she'd actually spelled out to him in advance that she didn't want her daugh-ter to know about their affair. Surely he would realise this without her having to put it into words?

The problem was, there was so much else they weren't putting into words at the moment. All yesterday, her voice had been rusty with fear and unshed tears, and he had seemed so withdrawn. He'd put her to bed at their bed-and-breakfast without saying more than a few words when they got back from Royal North Shore.

How could a man be so tender and so dis-tant, both at the same time? He'd brought her lunch on a tray, attractively prepared and set out by the B and B's ultra-professional hosts, Kevin and Joy Bradley. Then he'd left her to rest for the whole afternoon. Hadn't said where he was going.

Shopping, it turned out. He had brought her a gift of jewellery—an exquisite and expensive solid gold bracelet, inlaid with Australian opals that glinted with red, blue and purple fire.

'Steve…' she'd said with tears in her eyes. The colours in the milky stones had seemed to move with the movement of her wrist as she tried it on.

'Don't say anything. I know it's not enough. But I wanted to. Hell, I *needed* to!'

She'd kept it on for the rest of the day and was wearing it again now.

They had eaten take-away Italian food in their room and had watched the television that Joy Bradley had wheeled in during the afternoon. 'What a pity to get sick and spoil your break!' she had said.

This morning, it had been an effort to rise, pack and leave in time to be here at the airport for Maddy's dawn arrival. Neither of them had talked much. Candace had been too busy shovelling in crackers and sipping on bottled water. She hadn't felt this queasy for days.

I should have spelled it out to him, about us. I don't want Maddy to know.

Why? Her instinct on this niggled at her. Is our relationship something I'm ashamed of? Surely it can't be!

'Maddy, this is Dr Colton, who was nice enough to drive me up to meet your flight.' She avoided mentioning the fact that the drive had taken place three days ago, then remembered the evidence of two bulging overnight bags in the trunk of his car, and added, 'He...uh...showed me around Sydney, too.'

'Hi, Dr Colton.'

'Call me Steve.'

'Do I get to see around Sydney as well?'

'I'm afraid not, honey. Not this time. We have to head south.'

Maddy shrugged. 'Maybe when we come to pick up Grammy.' She yawned. 'I guess I need to sleep, anyway.'

She did a good bit of that on the journey south, and they didn't stop to eat or stretch their legs. Reaching Taylor's Beach, she was suddenly wide awake again, and open-mouthed about the location of Candace's house.

'*On* the beach, Mom! That's so cool!' Then her face fell. 'Only it's winter. How can it be winter? It's so warm!'

'People swim here all year round,' Steve offered.

'*Some* people,' Candace stressed, remembering Doreen Malvern's opinion on the issue.

'So cool!' Maddy repeated, and ran straight up the external stairs to check out the house, while Steve brought up her suitcases.

She was out on the ocean-facing deck when he was ready to leave. Candace didn't miss his cautious look in that direction, from his position at the top of the stairs, before he brushed her arm lightly with his fingers.

'When are we going to see each other?' he asked her quietly.

'I…hadn't thought.'

'She'll conk out pretty early tonight, won't she?' he pressed. 'How about if I come round?'

'All right.'

She didn't want to sound too eager, or let that 'number three—we have to talk' look that he teased her about appear on her face. Didn't want to scare him off. Not now. She *needed* him.

'I'll see you tonight, then.'

He craned to take another look through the open-plan living room and out to the deck, and was evidently satisfied that Maddy was still watching the ocean. His kiss came and went quickly, accompanied by the equally brief tangle of his fingers with hers.

Candace was left fighting the need to go after him.

Half to her surprise, she spent a great afternoon and early evening with Maddy. Her

daughter was less full of teenage prickles and
moods and cagey behaviour than she had been
a few months earlier when Candace had left
Boston. Perhaps three months of living with
Brittany and Todd had made her appreciate her
mother's better qualities!

Whatever the reason for it, Candace wal-
lowed unashamedly in the simple joy of her
daughter's company. Wished it could always
be like this—that they could always have a
fresh appreciation of each other.

She spoiled Maddy a little bit, too. They
picked up her current food fads from the supermarket, stopped at a fashion boutique and
bought her a new bikini and a wide-brimmed
hat. Even Candace's comment about the bikini
being the tiniest one in the store and yet the
most expensive was said half in fun and earned
only an unrepentant grin.

Back home, they walked north along the
beach to a little convenience store and bought
huge, chocolate-coated ice creams, talking all
the way.

It was so nice, just so nice, and it brought
back memories of so many other wonderful
times with Maddy over the fifteen and a half
years of her life that Candace found herself
thinking, I'd give anything if I could have this

again. If I could have another happy, healthy child...

After a simple meal, Maddy was in bed by eight o'clock. Candace waited a discreet half-hour, and was just about to phone Steve when she heard his footsteps—she always knew which ones were his—on the stairs.

'Maddy hasn't been in bed that long,' she warned him, jittery once more about the possibility of discovery.

'I could check that her light was off before I came up,' Steve reassured her, 'since her room fronts the street. But why are we whispering?'

She shrugged awkwardly. 'You know. Just in case.'

She made tea and he switched on the television, which earned her querying look.

'I don't like unnatural silence,' was his answer.

'Was it unnatural?'

'Bit.'

'I've...uh...got a pretty big list tomorrow,' she said, sounding too bright. 'Haven't done a Wednesday list before. What's Colin Ransome like to work with, do you know?'

'Slow, I gather. Super-cautious. Frustrates the nurses, but you can't fault him for wanting to be a hundred per cent sure of what he's doing. I guess a couple of times he's cancelled patients from my practice when I felt he could have gone ahead in perfect safety but, hey, I was the anaesthetist who ended up with Eric Kellett nearly falling victim to malignant hyperthermia.'

'That wasn't your fault. On what basis would Colin Ransome have decided to cancel surgery in that case? There were no indicators.' It was an effort to manufacture some energy about the issue.

'Is this what we want to talk about?' he said, with a sudden change of tone.

'No, of course not,' she answered. 'I was trying to deal with that unnatural silence.'

'Yeah, OK,' he agreed. 'I'm sorry. It's probably my fault. How are you feeling?'

'How do you think?'

He shook his head.

Silence. Achingly natural this time. There just wasn't anything to say. Nothing would help.

What would we do if...? How would you feel if...?

He had to be thinking of Helen and Matt, but their situation was very different. Not necessarily easier, or harder. No one could make that kind of comparison. But different.

They already had a commitment to each other which had stood the test of time and the births of three healthy children. They hadn't been faced with the uncertainty of waiting. They hadn't had a decision to make. They'd simply had to grieve. Together.

'Let's watch television,' Steve said finally. It was what they had both been doing, numbly, for fifteen minutes anyway.

He put his arm around her and she rested her head on his shoulder, as quiescent as a sleepy child. She tried to enjoy the simple, in-the-moment pleasure of it, the way she'd enjoyed Maddy's company today, but couldn't do it.

'Kiss me,' he whispered after a while, and bent his face to hers before she could reply. 'Please, kiss me. I'm hungry for you, Candace. I want to drown myself in your body, and not have to think.'

'Mmm...'

The little sound she made against his warm mouth was kittenish and pained at the same time. If their relationship had ever been simple, it wasn't any more. Winding her arms around his neck, she pulled him closer, seeking oblivion.

'Oh!'

The tiny, half-stifled cry came from a sleepy figure standing at the mouth of the short corridor which led to the two bedrooms. In a daze, Candace looked up in time to see Maddy turn on her heel and disappear, her pale, winter cotton nightdress belling around her legs. A moment later, the door of her room shut with a hollow bang.

'Damn!' Steve said succinctly.

'She only saw...' Candace began.

'She saw your blouse unfastened to the waist, my hands all over the place and my eyes closed because you feel too damned good for me to ever keep them open,' he retorted. 'That's quite a lot. You didn't want this to happen.'

It was a statement, not a question.

'No,' she agreed, and didn't elaborate because he seemed to understand without her explanation. 'It could have been worse. She could have seen us—'

'She's fifteen years old, armed with sex education and an imagination. She didn't need to actually see it,' he pointed out.

'Yes, look, I'd better—'

'Of course.' He nodded quickly. 'Go and sort it out. Talk about it. I don't mind what you tell her now. It's your call.'

'Thanks. I—I'll feel my way with it, I think.'

'I'll go, then.' He eased himself from the couch, letting his fingers trail lightly down her arm. 'Let me know whether we're…off the hook, or—'

'Off the hook?' she echoed on a taut laugh. 'You have a strange outlook at times.'

'Do I? What other times have I—?'

'No.' She shook her head. 'Don't take any notice, OK? It's me. My fault.'

Suddenly, Candace couldn't wait for him to leave, and was full of remorse that she'd let him come here tonight at all. This—all of it—everything—was overwhelming at the moment, and his presence was an additional and very emotional ingredient which didn't help.

'Just go, Steve,' she added. 'Please.'

'Sure.' He nodded. 'Sure, Candee.'

She was knocking on Maddy's door before he'd even reached the stairs.

'Can I come in, honey?'

There was no answer, but she heard movement and padding footsteps, and a moment later the door pulled open.

'You could have told me you were sleeping with him!' Maddy accused. Her body blocked the doorway defensively, and her voice was high and hard.

Candace didn't bother to deny the assumption, since it was entirely correct. 'Could I? I mean, *should* I?'

'Why, what was your plan? To have *that* happen?'

I didn't have a plan. I should have, but I didn't. There has been too much else to think about, and I can't tell you any of it yet. Not until I know...

'I'm sorry,' she blurted.

'Like, that's adequate?'

Where was the sunny, confiding friend from this afternoon? Vanished into thin air. And with some justification, perhaps.

'No, it isn't adequate,' Candace said steadily, 'but it happens to be true. I *am* sorry you had to find out about Steve that way.'

'I mean, what is it? Did it just start? You haven't mentioned him in your e-mails or your calls. Is he important, or is it just an affair? Like, a transitional relationship to get over

Dad, or something? It has to be, doesn't it? I mean, he's Australian, and you don't actually live here.'

Bombarded with every question she'd asked herself over the past few weeks, spoken in an unflagging tone of accusation, Candace's frayed nerves suddenly snapped.

'Please, don't speak to me that way,' she said crisply.

'Oh, I don't have the right to be told? You'd ask me some pretty pithy questions if you came across me half-naked in a guy's arms on the couch!'

'You have a right to ask the questions,' Candace conceded, her voice still sharp with anger. 'Just not in that way. And I don't promise that I have the answers. Not all of them.'

'So what answers do you have?'

'Uh…' Candace's silence was a crumbling cliff-edge all around the precarious piece of high ground she had retreated to. She took a deep, jagged breath. 'It didn't just start,' she said. 'It's been happening for a while.'

'What, you went to bed on the first date?'

'That's *enough*! I'm trying to talk to you like a rational human being. At least give me the space to do it! It's been happening for a while, and I don't—I can't tell you where it's going. Maybe it is just a "transitional relation-ship", as you put it. I was… Well, I was dev-astated by the way your father handled his de-parture, and— Look, I still don't know if I'm thinking straight, OK?'

'Is he going to be staying while I'm here?' Maddy ploughed on, ignoring Candace's plea for understanding and her attempt at a coher-ent, honest explanation. 'Am I going to have to *listen* to the two of you? Whistle or sing or stomp my feet before I enter a room in my own house in case a parent of mine is getting phys-ical in there with their new squeeze? God, I hoped I was getting *away* from that when I came out here!'

'*I—don't—know!*' Candace yelled, and burst into tears.

Maddy swore through her teeth, then held out her arms awkwardly. They hugged. Candace apologised, felt she should be han-dling all of this better but didn't know how.

'I mean,' Maddy went on, her voice now full of the appeal that betrayed how close she still was to childhood, 'do you really have to get married again, or be in another relation-ship, or whatever? Grammy never married again.'

'Grammy was sixty-four when your grand-father died,' Candace pointed out gently. 'I think that makes a difference, don't you? And "never" is a big word. It's only been four years.'

'I guess,' Maddy conceded. It was a token. 'Just don't spoil my vacation, OK? I've been so looking forward to this.'

'I won't spoil your vacation,' Candace replied in a tone of controlled patience, then wondered if she had the right to make such a promise when she had no idea how she was going to fulfil it.

'So, how'd it go?' Steve said, without moving his lips.

'Not great... Hi, Marion! You're quiet in here today.' Candace had to switch tone and mood suddenly at the older woman's approach.

'Don't jinx it!' answered Marion Lonergan, the sister in charge of the accident and emergency department at the hospital.

'OK, that's me caught up on notes,' Steve said, dropping his pen on the A and E office desk. 'If they can't get him up to the ward, Marion, let me know, OK?'

He handed a patient file back to Sister Lonergan.

Candace smiled automatically, not taking any of it in. She wasn't interested in this patient, an emergency admission. She just wanted to talk to Steve with a degree of privacy. Perhaps it had been crazy to even attempt it in the middle of the A and E department. He was on call in here today, while she was in between the first and second patients on her own surgical list.

'She was hostile, or what?' Steve asked, returning to the subject that concerned them as soon as Marion Lonergan had left the small office.

'Hostile,' Candace confirmed. 'Selfish. Kind of ''Why do I have to be inconvenienced?'' sort of thing, but she had a point. Kids of her age find this stuff hugely embarrassing between people over the age of about nineteen. She has to deal with Todd and Brittany at home, and she hates it. She wants to live with my mother when she goes back, and I'm starting to think it's a good idea. She and Mom adore each other. I should have thought about how we were going to handle it, but then the issue of the baby came up and...' She felt a familiar lump swell in her throat.

'Should we take a break, then?' he suggested.

Candace's stomach dropped.

'A break,' she echoed stupidly.

'If you're concerned that it will be difficult for her,' he explained in a helpful tone.

'Right. Yes. I understand.' She leaned her splayed fingers on the desk and sat down slowly, battled not to betray the way her legs had suddenly drained of strength. 'Yes, I guess that's the easiest thing.'

'I mean, your mother is coming in two weeks and I imagine you might find it even harder to deal with her—'

'Yes,' she repeated, cutting him off. 'I take your point. Yes. Let's take a break.'

'Rather than having to sneak off and make excuses. We've both been doing enough of that as it is, wanting to keep this private from our colleagues.'

'*Yes!* I'm not arguing, am I? It makes sense. Stop bombarding me with reasons, Steve!'

'Sorry.'

'God, why are we always apologising to each other these days?' she hissed in an undertone, lurching to her feet and stumbling for the door.

He didn't follow her. Perhaps he was afraid they'd create too much of a scene. Perhaps he had another reason. She didn't know.

Back outside Theatres, she picked up the phone, pressed some buttons at random, with the heel of her hand holding down the disconnect button—fortunately no one was watching—and said brightly to the dial tone, 'Yes, I'll hold.'

Then she sat with the buzzing phone against her ear and yesterday's newspaper blurring in her vision, simply buying time. Time to regain control enough to go on with surgery. She had three more procedures scheduled this morning. The nurses were still cleaning up Theatre One after the last patient and preparing for the next, but he was here waiting on a stretcher already, and it wouldn't be long before she was needed.

I can't! I didn't want Steve to say that!

Take a break? *Now?* When our baby might have Down's, and I have to suffer through maybe nearly three more weeks before we know? I need Steve. We need each other, don't we? Obviously he doesn't think we do, or he would have bent over backwards to find a way to ride it out together until Maddy and Mom leave.

Lord, I wanted the two of them here so much! I was so thrilled to see Maddy and now, already, I'm wishing she was gone. Counting the days. No! I don't want Maddy gone, I want both of them. Her and Steve.

Damn it, you fool, you've fallen in love with him, haven't you?

The realisation entered her mind as if it had been spoken by someone else.

I'm in love with him.

I wasn't ready for it *at all*, but it's happened anyway. Is it just because I'm carrying his baby? No, it's not. I would have felt it anyway.

And now we're not going to see each other—not in any way that counts—until Mom and Maddy leave.

If then.

Maybe this is his way of breaking it off. He's easing me out of it by talking about taking a break until Maddy leaves, but once that happens, he'll deal the final blow.

All at once, everything in Steve's behaviour over the past few days crystallised into a new, meaningful picture that she hadn't picked up on before. His silence and his aura of preoccupation. The expensive piece of jewellery he had given her.

She wasn't wearing the gold bangle today, because she was operating. It sat in its box in her top drawer at home, lovingly placed there last night when she'd taken it off before bed. She had been so thrilled and warmed about the gift, and only now realised that she'd subconsciously interpreted it as a love token, a sign of their shared tribulation, a symbol of all the things that were too hard, for both of them, to put into words.

But perhaps it wasn't that at all.

Not a love token. A prelude to goodbye. Something to sweeten the pill, because Steve had realised he couldn't handle it any more. She was going to be on her own...

'You poor thing, are you still on hold?' Robyn Wallace said, coming over to the desk to write up the current recovery patient's chart.

Candace jumped and realised that the dial tone was still buzzing in her ear.

'Oh... Yes... I'll have to try again another time,' she said feebly, and broke the connection.

Her next patient had been wheeled in, and they would be ready for her as soon as she'd scrubbed.

But she had forgotten that this wasn't Steve Colton on anaesthesia today. Steve had been right. Colin Ransome was slow. Used to the anaesthesiologists she worked with in Boston, with many years of specialist expertise under their belts, she had to fight not to snap at him and the atmosphere in Theatre One was much more tense than usual.

'Are you feeling all right?' Doreen asked her at one point.

'Fine. Just tired. I was so thrilled about Maddy arriving, I hardly slept last night,' she lied glibly, then wondered how many more lies she'd have to tell, to how many more people, over the coming weeks.

CHAPTER EIGHT

'So, WHAT can I do for you today, Andrea?' Steve asked.

It was an effort to focus on his work at the moment. He was racked with guilt and longing, and didn't know how to make it go away. A part of him wanted to run a mile.

If this is what Matt means when he tells me I need to 'get serious', he can keep it for himself! If this is part of the job description, then I'm woefully underqualified. Who needs to feel this way, day in and day out? It isn't fun! From the beginning, something told me to tread carefully with this one, only I didn't do it. Not really. Now I'm in deep enough to drown...

To drown in Candace's tired, pain-filled eyes. To drown in her trembling body, in the cool sweetness of her voice, in their rambling, teasing conversations.

And it doesn't feel good. What I'm feeling at the moment just doesn't feel good.

'I'm moving to Sydney,' Andrea Johnson was saying, as he forced himself to focus. 'Just thought that after what happened in March, I should have a thorough check-up first.'

'Yes, that's sensible.' He remembered her emergency surgery for appendicitis, and the benign tumour that had been removed instead. He read the details in Candace's handwriting in Andrea's notes. 'You'll need to find a good GP in Sydney once you're settled. I can recommend a couple of names.'

'I don't know whereabouts I'll be living yet,' she said. 'It's all a bit of a leap in the dark.'

'You don't have a job to go to?'

'No, but with my computer skills it shouldn't be difficult.'

'Let's have a look at you, then.'

He ran through the usual things. Her blood pressure was fine, nice and low at 110 over 70. Chest and heart sounded good. Clear lungs, healthy heart rhythm and pulse. He asked her a couple of general questions, then did a pap smear, and she was a young, confident woman who wasn't put off by his gender, during what some women considered a horribly intimate procedure.

With a patient's lower body concealed behind a sheet and with most of the work done by feel, Steve found pap smears to be just part of the routine. He chatted a little to help her relax, warmed the speculum with his hands and obtained the cell samples without difficulty. Then he dealt with the slide, disposed of his gloves and left the treatment room so that Andrea could get dressed again.

When she reappeared, he said, 'We should just run through a couple more things. You've had no trouble with your incision as it's healed?'

'It itches sometimes, but that's all. My sister Carina says hers does, too. Only, of course, she has a baby to show for her scar, so everyone's a lot more sympathetic and interested!'

She laughed, but it was a rather bitter sound. Steve waited and, sure enough, there was more.

'That's why I'm moving to Sydney,' she went on.

'Because of Carina, and people fussing over the baby?'

'Because I'm sick of putting myself through it. It's my fault. I know that. Carina's OK. She doesn't mean to rub it in my face that she's got a husband and a baby and all that, but...' She trailed off, then shrugged. 'You know, I just want to get away. Go somewhere where I don't have to feel like this.'

'Yeah, I know what you mean.'

Better than you realise. I'd like to go somewhere where I don't have to feel like this, too.

Guessing that she might regret giving away too much, he went on in a different tone, 'Give the front desk a ring early next week for the pap-smear result. Do you have any other health concerns at the moment?'

'No, I feel fighting fit. If this move works out—'

'Yes, good luck with it. Maybe I'll hear from Carina how you're doing.'

After Andrea had gone, Steve worked his way through a steady stream of patients for the rest of the day and left his practice just before six, feeling exhausted. Totally exhausted. Not physically, which he always considered to be a healthy feeling, but mentally. Emotionally. And it was only Monday!

A week since Candace's test. Another two weeks before they could reliably expect the results. Five days since he'd suggested taking a break.

Was that for her or for me? he wondered as he took a jog along the beach in the dark after he reached home to try and pound out some of the frustration. I thought I was thinking of her, but maybe I'm kidding myself. Maybe I just can't handle the guilt...

He hardly felt the cold foam of the waves around his feet and calves, hardly saw the cliffs and the houses, looming against a clear, starry sky, or the pieces of tangled, scrubby bush. He ran until his lungs ached sharply, and his bare ears were almost numbed by the salt wind.

The guilt.

It had been *his* contraceptive which had failed. Should he have told her at the time that he'd sensed something wasn't quite right, that he'd suspected a tear in the paper-thin latex? He hadn't been sure. If it had been a tear, it had been a tiny one. What did you do? Put the thing under a magnifying glass? So early in their relationship, he hadn't wanted to be neurotic about it.

And it was *his* family's recent experience which had cast such a dark cloud over the ambiguous picture of the baby on the scan. Down's syndrome was a challenge to deal with as an abstract possibility, but for many families there was a positive outcome in the end. He knew Helen and Matt would have made it work if their baby had lived. But little Robbie had been too weak to survive, and it brought all those abstract questions into stark focus.

I yelled at her about it, he remembered, when she asked what I thought about testing. I told her of course I was thinking about Matt and Helen and Robbie, made *her* think about them, too.

He slowed to a walk, his chest heaving, and bent forward with his hands on his knees for a moment to catch his breath. His lungs felt half-frozen, and his ears began to ache at once as feeling returned painfully.

Just ahead, the lights of the houses blinked through the gnarled shapes of the banksia trees like the rhythmic blink of the lighthouse on a distant headland to the north. The wind had freshened, and the trees were swaying, cutting back and forth through the beams of warm yellow.

He knew which lights belonged to Candace's house. She was economical about light herself, and kept a room dark if she wasn't in it. Maddy was apparently more careless. Every room was lit up, and the place beckoned like a siren's cave.

He might have liked Maddy if he'd had a chance to get to know her. She was at the prickliest of stages, and would remain there for a couple more years before her perspective matured. She was a factor to consider—a factor that Candace was, no doubt, considering obsessively.

He almost went up and hammered on their door, but then thought better of it. They'd agreed on 'a break'. His word, but he was sorry he'd used it now. Candace hadn't even phoned, and he just wanted to hear her voice. Hell, so badly! It needn't be a long conversation. Just to touch base, say to each other, 'I'm still alive.'

Well, of course, he knew she was still alive! He was seeing her in surgery tomorrow.

But he hadn't meant that to be their only contact. He'd meant taking a break from sleeping together, from spending their time with each other, so that Candace wouldn't have to deal with Maddy's teenage sensitivity on the issue of adult sexuality at a time when she particularly wanted things to run smoothly with her daughter.

Yes, I *was* thinking of her, he realised. But now I'm thinking of me. I miss her far more than I want to...

'I'm going to use mesh. Look, this area on the opposite side is pretty weak, too. That's recent.

There's no sense in pushing it back in here only to have it pop out the other side in six months' time. Or six days, when he has a good cough! You're doing fine, Mr Gatto,' Candace told the unconscious patient, 'but we're going to have to talk about your job.'

The patient's weight and habits, too, Steve observed. Arno Gatto had clocked in at 143 kilograms this morning, and Steve was dosing him accordingly. Mr Gatto had taken an unusually long time to close his eyes and sink into the oblivion of the anaesthesia.

He worked at a local lumber yard, in a job that involved frequent lifting, but this didn't mean he was fit or healthy. He was a heavy smoker, and from the smell of his hair, even through his disposable cap, he hadn't completely stopped before the surgery as Candace, his GP, Peter Moody and Doreen Malvern, during the pre-admission clinic, would all have advised him to do.

'Hang in there, everyone, we'll be taking a little longer than expected,' Candace said.

'What's up?' Peter himself was assisting with surgery, and he seemed a little tense and jumpy, as if he was wondering if the pre-admission check-up on his patient had been thorough enough.

'We have a hernia textbook here,' Candace answered lightly.

'A textbook hernia?'

'No, I said a hernia textbook. What's that line from *Oklahoma!* about "bustin' out all over"?'

Steve grinned, and couldn't wipe the expression off his face. He shook his head and looked back at his monitors. Despite everything that was going on, Tuesday was still the best day of the week as far as he was concerned.

Candace had relaxed in surgery over the past few months. Not too much. Nothing out of character. She still didn't want music or gossip or anything that distracted from her focus, but she made almost every procedure interesting, and there was something almost artistic in the way she moved. Her neat hands, the way she bent her head, the uncurling of her wrist as she reached for an instrument.

The tight, pale gloves emphasised the grace of the gesture, and Steve often caught himself watching her hands far too intently.

'What are you going to do?' Peter was asking.

'I'm going to illustrate the proverb "A stitch in time saves nine" and deal with the weakness on the other side, too. Will he handle it, Steve?'

'On current indications, yes, and that's certainly what pre-admission suggested, isn't it, Doreen? Peter? Strong as an ox, aren't you, Mr Gatto?'

'That's what I told you, Dr Fletcher,' Peter said. 'But I think Mr Gatto takes that a bit too much for granted. He gets away with a lifestyle that would have killed a lot of people years ago, don't you, Mr G.? I wonder if he cut down on his smoking at all?'

'Pat, better tell them outside that we won't be done in here before...' Candace glanced at the clock '...noon, I'd say. Mr Gatto, we're going to give you a nicotine patch and chest physio and extra abdominal support after this. Can't have you coughing all my stitches out, can we? That would give new meaning to what my daughter says about coughing when she has a chest infection.'

'Stop it, Dr Fletcher, you're making me laugh,' Steve growled, and their eyes met for a moment.

He saw the way hers brightened, saw the self-conscious flush in her cheeks as it crept above the top of her mask. She flicked her gaze down again, and said with a change of tone,

'Blood in the surgical field has darkened, Steve. How's his oxygen?'

'OK, a bit low.' He adjusted the level, the calm of his manner a little deceptive.

'Temp?'

'Normal. Heart's normal.'

'Lord, are we still jittery after Eric Kellett?' Doreen voiced the concern they'd all felt for a moment. 'What would those odds be? To have another malignant hyperthermia crisis so soon?'

'Slim,' Candace agreed.

'Odds don't work that way in medicine,' Steve pointed out.

'Some people win the lottery twice,' Peter agreed. 'Candace, the pre-admission assessment on this patient—*my* assessment, before he even got to the clinic, and his clinic visit as well—wasn't based on his fitness for a double operation.'

'I know,' she said. 'But ultimately it's less stressful this way than putting him under twice. What's it called? An economy of scale, or something? Both sides at once doesn't take nearly as long as two sides separately. I know what I'm doing, and I'll work as efficiently as I can. Steve, if there's the slightest sign that this is too much for him, let me know and we'll bail out, OK? I can schedule a second procedure if I have to.'

'No worries, Dr Fletcher,' he said, then took his usual pleasure in watching the way she worked. Those hands, the angle of her head and her eyes squinting in concentration.

They'd almost reached the end of the procedure when Mr Gatto's heart tracing went haywire, then flattened to nothing, accompanied by the high-pitched monotone of the alarm. They had equipment on hand, and everyone took their assigned roles with a smoothness that would have made Steve feel a little smug about his rural Australian hospital—if he'd had the time to feel anything.

The paddles pressed to Mr Gatto's chest were brutal in their effect. His torso arched up from the operating table, then slumped down heavily, his solid flesh shaking.

'Nothing,' Steve reported through tight lips. 'Let's go again.'

They gave it a bigger charge this time, and inside the cage of those comfortably padded ribs the heart responded at last. The rhythm on the monitor was erratic at first, but quickly settled and steadied.

'OK, I'm breathing again,' Candace muttered.

Steve followed up quickly with drugs to maintain blood pressure and the correct rhythm, and she put her final sutures in place without saying another word.

Out in Recovery, he ached to follow her out to the tearoom. Was that where she'd gone? She wasn't here on the phone, using the space between patients to catch up on other business as she often did. He knew he couldn't go in search of her, though.

He wasn't prepared to leave anything to chance now, and stayed at the patient's side until he was confident that Mr Gatto was emerging from the anaesthesia as he should. His big frame looked like an empty shell, and his recovery would be slow and uncertain.

Is Candace blaming herself? Steve wondered, staring at the ECG monitor that was still tracking Mr Gatto's heart rhythm. She was right to handle it the way she did. These things happen, and she fixed both those hernias in less than the time it would have taken Harry Elphick to do one of them, particularly in those last few years before he retired. Where's she got to, I wonder?

He would have liked to have talked to her. He remembered that other time when they'd got Eric Kellett through his malignant hyperthermia crisis by the skin of their teeth, and she'd then forgotten to give the next patient a local anaesthetic to tide the woman through the first few hours after her painful haemorrhoidectomy and vein-stripping.

Then, Candace had expressed her need for Steve with a clinging touch on his arm and a huge-eyed gaze. This time, during the routine vasectomy that followed, an hour later than scheduled, she didn't even look his way.

He waited at home that night quite deliberately. Listened for the phone while he made scrambled eggs on toast for dinner. Didn't take a shower in case she phoned while he was in there and he didn't hear over the sound of running water.

But when it did ring, a little later, it was only Helen, inviting him for a family dinner at the weekend. After that, he got impatient and angry—with Candace? He went out to a late movie that he didn't particularly want to see, because if Candace hadn't phoned by five past nine, then she probably wasn't going to phone at all, and he was damned if he'd spend the entire evening waiting by the phone like a teenage girl.

If she didn't need him, fine. If his instinct about the strength of what she felt at the moment was wrong, fine. He wasn't enjoying this, anyway.

Like Andrea Johnson yesterday, he was sick of putting himself through it.

Did that mean he was giving up? That he was ready to abandon Candace, their conceived-too-soon baby and their no-strings-attached relationship?

No! No, he *wasn't* giving up, and sooner rather than later Candace needed to know it.

CHAPTER NINE

'I FEEL as if I've let you down terribly by not having you over before this,' Myrna Davis said to Candace. 'After you were so helpful in getting Terry and me settled in during his fellowship stint in Boston all those years ago.'

'Don't be silly, Myrna. You shouldn't have felt that you needed to do it even now.'

They were seated together in a paved area of garden at the back of the Davises' attractive house, overlooking the river estuary. Terry was flourishing an expensive set of barbecue tongs over a smoking grill, and the June sunshine was stronger and warmer than winter sun had any right to be. There were about twenty people present, and they were all enjoying themselves.

'This is one of my good weeks, between cycles,' Myrna said. 'Now that I know the pattern, I can leave my chemotherapy weeks blank and slot things into the times I know I'll be feeling well.'

'That sounds far too sensible, Myrna! Are you looking after yourself properly?'

'No choice in that department.' The older woman laughed. 'I knew that chemo hits a lot of people hard, but somehow hadn't expected to have to cart a bucket and a box of tissues around with me at every step!'

'Oh, heavens, yes, you poor thing!'

Candace's sympathy was coloured by her own current situation. Myrna was trying to be funny about it, and Candace appreciated the other woman's courage in making light of the ongoing threat to her health, but even the wittiest observations on intractable nausea hit far too close to home at the moment.

She'd been feeling worse over the past couple of days than she had felt a week ago, even though she'd reached the thirteen-week mark, when most women began to feel somewhat better as their hormones stabilised.

It was stress and fatigue, Candace knew. She wasn't sleeping well, couldn't relax by day or by night with the test result still likely to be a week away or more. She was trying hard to ensure that Maddy had a good time, but that took effort as well. She didn't always want to go to a movie or to the local shopping mall after work.

Linda Gardner's teenagers were helping enormously, at least. Richard was seventeen and Julia was just a few months younger than Maddy, and Candace had hosted a casual evening of pizza and ice cream the previous weekend, to which both of them had brought friends.

It was surprising how much clearing up there was to do after ten teenagers when you hadn't even cooked for them, but apparently it had been worth the effort. Richard and Julia and a couple of their friends were here at the Davises' today, and Maddy had hardly deigned to talk to anyone else.

One less thing to worry about.

That wasn't necessarily a plus. In her churning mind, Steve Colton quickly stretched out a little further to fill the newly available space.

He was stretching out now, on one of the Davises' outdoor jarrah-wood chairs near the barbecue grill—legs straight at the knee and crossed at the ankles, fingers laced behind his head and elbows pressed back, casual knit shirt hugging tight across his broad chest.

Not a care in the world? she wondered.

His eyes were closed. His face was basking in the sun's gentle caress. He looked like an itinerant surfer, tanned and free and immortal.

Then she looked closer, and saw the frown notched into his forehead, and the way those closed lids narrowed and flickered. He wasn't really relaxing. He was just wishing he could.

Don't get it wrong, she chided herself. He's in this with me at least as far as the baby's health is concerned. He'll help.

How much help can you give from ten thousand miles away?

It's not his fault that I've fallen in love with him. That was never part of the deal. I'm the one who has changed the rules.

Had he felt her watching him? His lids flickered again then opened, and he sat up straight and shielded his eyes with his hand. Her gaze clashed with his, and he gave a quick, covert smile that was too wry and too complicated.

Her heart did a backward somersault inside her chest. Or maybe it was her stomach. Whichever organ was involved in the uncomfortable sensation, it would win a gold medal in gymnastics at the next Olympic Games at this rate. It was certainly training hard!

'Sausages and steaks are up,' Terry announced. 'Satay sticks are about two minutes away. Help yourselves, everyone. Salads on the table, meats over here.'

Candace got up to grab a plate before Myrna could make a fuss over her. She hated feeling like the guest of honour. Everyone must have been hungry, because a line had formed already, with the teenagers at the head of it and several adults hard on their heels.

Coming next, Candace knew it was Steve who stood behind her, without even turning her head to look. A few moments later, they stood side by side at the salad table, and when his bare arm brushed hers as he leaned towards the coleslaw, she knew it was deliberate, a caress that said, I'm still here. I haven't disappeared.

Yes, but only under the terms of the original agreement, she wanted to answer his unworded message. I want so much more than that now.

Did she, though?

She heard Maddy's confident yet still endearingly childlike laugh. 'Richard, that is *so gross*!'

What *do* I want? My life isn't here, it's halfway around the world. That's where I have a career. Status and office staff, an extremely healthy income and a very large house, with Todd's share in it ceded to me under the terms of our divorce. More importantly, *most* importantly, that's where I have friends I feel truly comfortable with, and a mother I love, and a daughter who's the light of my life. Does loving Steve mean that I'd give all that up to stay here if he asked?

Loving Steve...

It was an instinct at the moment. A need. It made perfect, crystal-clear sense of some things, but threw others into total confusion. Little, trivial things such as her entire future.

'Have Terry and Myrna shown you their garden yet?' Steve said to Candace in his 'public' voice, the one he used to her in front of colleagues, or in front of Maddy, or at any time when he thought they might be overheard.

'No, they haven't,' she answered, in her own version of the same thing.

She wondered if hers grated on his nerves as much as his did on hers. Her public voice was too high-pitched, too cooing and polite, while his was exaggeratedly Aussie, like that of some lone wolf Outback type who'd never had a sexual thought about an older woman in his life.

Dear God, the age thing! She hadn't even given a thought to that potential problem for a while, because it seemed so trivial against all the rest. But maybe it counted against both of them, too, counted against any possibility of a long-term future together.

Women matured earlier than men, and had a head start. At least she'd lived and suffered. Suffered through the slow, unnoticed deterioration of a marriage, the bitterness of betrayal and divorce, the indescribable joys and relentless fears of parenthood. Steve was getting a crash course in the last item, and maybe, at thirty-three, he just wasn't ready for it.

'Eat your lunch and I'll take you on a tour,' he offered heartily.

'That sounds lovely...' she squeaked and cooed in reply.

Her appetite had fled, but she downed a small plate of salad and barbecued meat. Steve poured her some fruit juice and they wandered off together, glasses in hand, with Steve uttering loud, helpful comments about the terraced flower-beds and the native shrubbery. Candace looked back once, but Maddy hadn't even noticed she'd gone.

'They have a garden bench down here with great views of the water.'

'I think you can stop now, Steve.'

'I didn't want—' he began.

'I know.' She nodded, meeting him halfway. 'I do it, too, don't I? It's OK.'

They reached the bench but didn't sit on it. Candace put her empty glass down on a stone wall and stood awkwardly. There was a garden lamp just near the bench, and a set of stone steps running down to a small wooden dock where a small motorboat was moored.

'Lovely!' she murmured, leaning a hand on the black metal of the lamppost.

'You haven't phoned,' Steve said abruptly. 'Not once. In eleven days.'

She turned, taken aback by the accusation and suddenly hot with feeling. '*I* haven't phoned?'

'It's easier for you.'

His hands were folded across his chest, emphasising the hard strength of his forearms. She longed to stroke them as she had done so many times before, loving their raw, unmistakable masculinity. But she could tell he was angry, and it was like some sci-fi force field, keeping her at bay. She hadn't seen him like this before. His powerful physical energy had always manifested itself in other ways.

'The timing, I mean,' he went on. 'You know when Maddy won't be around to hear you. And you know I live alone. You're safe ringing my place pretty much any time you want. But you haven't.'

She was still bewildered at his attack, sick with it. 'You talked about taking a break,' she said helplessly. 'I didn't know you wanted me to phone.'

'Taking a break didn't have to mean total silence, did it?' His voice rasped harshly, and his blue eyes blazed.

'Did it? You tell me!'

'Well, it didn't. Not to me, it didn't.'

'I thought that was what you wanted.'

'No.' He swore under his breath.

'Do you think I've found it easy? Going through this alone?' Her voice rose. 'The endless, agonising wait, while I try to make things nice for Maddy and pretend everything's just fine and dandy. I feel like some demented kindergarten teacher, most days. ''Whoo-hoo, let's all have fun!'' While really I wish I could just crawl away somewhere and go into a deep sleep until this was *over*.' Her voice cracked on the word. 'And the only person who's in this too—you, Steve—has said to me that we're taking a break. I thought it was what you wanted,' she repeated.

'No, Candace. Hell, of course I wanted to keep in contact! I haven't dropped into a black hole.'

'You should have made it clearer.'

'I'm making it clear now.'

'OK...' She nodded thinly.

'Is that good enough?' he demanded.

'If that's what you're offering.'

'I'm still here, and I'm still this baby's father. I thought you understood that.'

'Yes… There's no fathering to be done at this point, is there?'

She didn't fully understand why she was pushing him away like this. Self-defence, maybe. Illogical, certainly. She was still reeling from the suddenness of his attack, although she'd started to understand his reasons now. But to feel herself in his arms now that she knew she loved him would surely be pain more than pleasure.

'What are you saying, Candace?' he growled. 'What do you mean by "at this point"? That baby's just as real to me as it is to you.'

'It isn't,' she argued. 'It can't be. You haven't felt its effect on your body. And you haven't had a child before. At least, not that you've mentioned. Perhaps there is one, tucked away somewhere?'

'Hey!' Steve took a lunging step forward and gripped her arms. His face blazed with anger. 'Hell, what is this?'

'You started it. I "haven't phoned". Like it was a deliberately inflicted wound.'

'I'm sorry. I was too abrupt. But, damn it, Candace...! And you're wrong! Don't you think it might be *harder* for me because I've never had a child, and because it's not a part of my body? I'm at sea. I'm totally powerless. Can't even pat my stomach the way you do, as a statement of love. I can do *nothing*, except stay away, and wait, and hope you'll take the initiative and phone. Do you know what it's like for a man when he has to do *nothing*? And you tell me you've got it hard?'

He shook his head, twisted on his feet, thrust his hands into his pockets and began to pace the little terrace as if he wished it were ten times the size. He didn't look at her. Did he know how closely she was watching him? She blinked back tears, and several painful questions hovered on her lips.

Is this the end? Are we calling it quits? Am I on my own?

Finally he stopped, turned, faced her.

'Are we giving up? Is that what we're saying?' she forced herself to ask.

For such huge questions, her voice was tiny, squeaky with unshed tears. Evidently, they had the power to electrify him into action.

'Giving up?' he echoed. 'Good God, Candee, no!'

He had gathered her against him before she had time to harden herself and fight him off.

They held each other rather desperately. He buried his face in the curve of her neck, and she felt the pleasing roughness of his jaw against her softer skin. She had her hair loosely swept back into a clip today, tumbling down between her shoulder blades. He laced its silky strands through his fingers, then took a ragged breath and began to kiss her hungrily, holding her against him with his hands bracketing her hips.

'Lord, I need this!' he muttered.

As always, it felt so right. It was the place she wanted to be. She needed the way he felt, and the way he smelt. She needed the sound of his voice vibrating in his chest when she pressed against its broad expanse and listened with one ear.

Not anyone else. Him. He was different to any other man. This was different to how she'd ever felt with Todd.

Better. More intense. More magical.

Candace felt the insistence of his arousal nudging against the heat of her groin and the push of her breasts against his chest, and it was so sweet, so *necessary*, when she hadn't touched him for more than ten days, that she

could only give in to it, drink it up and hold
onto it.

'You sounded very certain just now,' she
managed to whisper.

'Of course I'm certain!' he whispered huskily back. 'Do you think I'm going to walk
away from this just because we're having a
trivial fight?'

'It's not trivial, is it? We both said some
harsh things.'

'We're both under a lot of strain.' Steve
brushed his nose across hers, then drank hungrily from her lips, closed his eyes and slid his
hands up her bare thighs, taking her skirt with
him so that its light, billowy folds screened the
intimate movements of his fingers against her
body.

'And what's "this", Steve? You said you
needed "this".'

He stilled, took his hands away. Her skirt
fell. 'This,' he said. 'What we have.'

'What do we have?' She took a deep breath,
which she willed to be steady.

'Why do I have to answer that?' he returned
impatiently. 'And why do I have to answer it
now? Do you have an answer? We have this
intensity, this way of getting on with each
other... We have a baby coming, who might

need a huge amount of extra care. We have lives in opposite hemispheres.'

'Yes, and—'

'And against all that, we have this. *This!* I don't know what it is! If you have a suggestion, a definition, then I'm all ears.'

'I—I don't,' she admitted.

'So don't expect answers from me! I'm thinking one day—one *hour*—at a time at the moment. I try and think beyond the test result, but I can't. Can you?'

'No. But, Steve, I've made my decision.' There was both defiance and appeal in her voice.

Candace loosed herself from his arms, stepped back and lifted her head, waiting for him to ask what her decision was.

He didn't. He just watched her for a moment and nodded slowly. Following the downward flick of his gaze, she realised that he didn't need to ask. Her body language said it all. Unconsciously, she had flattened one hand across her lower stomach. He'd mentioned the gesture just a few moments ago. She was protecting their child as she would protect it from now on, no matter what.

Would she be protecting it alone? Neither of them knew.

I was crazy to think I'd be able do it, she chided herself. Immerse myself in him the way I did, and still walk away, untouched, when my year was up, taking our memories with me like a stack of photo albums.

Even if I hadn't got pregnant I couldn't have done it. Even if the very worst happens, and the test does show something so seriously and fatally wrong that we do opt for a termination, my awareness of it will always be there. We created a baby together. We suffered through this wait together.

'What you said about not phoning...' she said slowly.

'Probably wasn't fair,' he conceded.

'I guess I've still felt connected to you even when we haven't talked. Because I knew you had to be still thinking about it. When I saw you in surgery on Tuesday, it was obvious your nights have been as sleepless as mine.'

'Next time you're awake at two in the morning, come over and throw some pebbles against my window,' he teased. 'I'll be waiting.'

'Couldn't I just come to the front door?' Her laugh was almost a sob.

'Whatever you want, Candace,' he said. 'I just need you, OK? I'm not defining it, I'm not quantifying it. But I need you.'

So they got through the rest of the barbecue and the rest of the day, and she sneaked out that night when Maddy was asleep and went to Steve's place. They made love in front of some terrible fifty-year-old B movie on late night television, said all the same things they'd said to each other before, drank some hot chocolate and then just held each other.

And the holding was the only thing that really counted.

Elaine West was one of the last passengers off her flight to emerge from Customs the following Friday morning. As always, however, she emerged immaculate in every detail, from her tiny diamond earrings to her Italian leather shoes. At sixty-eight, in black trousers, a silk blouse, an elegant jacket and the perfect scarf, she was, as ever, the best-dressed woman Candace knew.

'No, the flight wasn't horrible at all,' she insisted airily after they'd hugged with greedy pressure. 'It's all common sense. Drink lots of fluids and walk up and down the aisles. Besides, I got an upgrade to first class,' she finished with a guilty smile, just when Candace was about to conclude that her mother really was inhumanly poised and perfect.

'So you really didn't need a weekend in a nice hotel in Sydney to recover before we drive down to Narralee?' Candace enquired deliberately.

An iron grip landed on her wrist.

'Darling, believe me, I need the hotel,' Elaine said. 'And it has to be a *proper* hotel, you know that, don't you? Not one of those ghastly bed-and-breakfasts that you like. I want anonymity and room service, not hand-quilted cushions. I've got those at home.'

Candace grinned. 'Don't worry, it's all taken care of. Maddy and I stayed there last night as well.'

'You'll love it, Grammy, and it's on the nineteenth floor,' Maddy said.

The further from the ground, the better, as far as Elaine was concerned.

'So we can go straight there?'

'Yes.'

'And you can freshen up a little, too.'

A pair of sharp black eyes alighted critically on Candace's worst features. The face that was innocent of make-up, showing its lines of strain starkly. The comfortable jeans she'd worn to drive up here last night, and hadn't bothered to replace with something smarter this morning. The hair that could have done with much more than a quick, vigorous brush, twist and clip high on the back of her head.

'You look terrible,' Elaine added, just in case her previous comment and her pointed regard had been too subtle.

Candace caught Maddy's startled glance and her sudden frown. Teenagers weren't the most observant people in the world, but they could use their eyes when they were pointed in the right direction, as Elaine had just done.

'I didn't find the pillows very comfortable last night,' Candace lied, and hoped her daughter wouldn't think back and realise that this peaky, strained appearance and casual approach to grooming had been in place for her entire stay.

'Hmm,' Elaine said. 'We'll call Housekeeping as soon as we get to the hotel and ask them to send up a different kind. And you've lost weight.'

'Yes, isn't it great?' Candace parried the accusation by changing the direction of its spin. 'With the beach right out front of my house, I'm getting so fit!'

She waited for a moment, her breath held tight in her chest, then let the air out with controlled relief when, without further comment on the subject, Elaine turned to her single suitcase.

'Maddy, you can get that for me, honey. It isn't heavy. It has another one nesting inside it for when I've shopped. Which we'll do this afternoon, shall we?'

Her beam of anticipation assumed enthusiastic agreement.

And after these first few awkward minutes, everything was fine. Back in their two-bedroom suite at the high-rise hotel, Maddy watched daytime soaps while Candace 'tried out the new pillows' and Elaine unpacked. They ordered an elegant brunch through room service, then embarked upon a serious shopping expedition.

Elaine expected Candace to be an expert on the city's most appealing merchandise but, of course, she wasn't, and in the end she let her mother take control. Translating the price tags into US currency, Elaine considered virtually everything to be a bargain, and they returned to the hotel at four o'clock with so many bags that she would have needed three suitcases nesting inside each other in order to fit everything in on the return flight.

'You can box the rest up for me and mail it back,' she told her daughter.

After two hours of serious rest and freshening up, they went to the revolving restaurant high above the city in Centrepoint Tower for drinks and dinner. Knowing that her mother would expect a high degree of elegance and finish, Candace wore heels and make-up, jewellery glinting here and there and hair in a proper French pleat. For the first time in weeks she actually felt good.

Energised. Optimistic. Safe. There was something about Elaine West's approach to life.

Or perhaps it's just because she's my mother, the one who's never let me down, in all these years...

'I'm so glad you came, Mom,' she whispered in a foggy voice, and put her arms around Elaine in the elevator going up to the restaurant. A subtle waft of cool, faint perfume reached her nostrils as Elaine returned the hug.

'We'll talk later, darling,' she promised. 'And you can tell me all about it.'

Which was almost as good as all those times in Candace's childhood when she'd heard in that same tender voice, 'It's all right, Candy, darling, Mommy will kiss it better.'

Obviously, Elaine knew perfectly well it wasn't just the hotel pillows that were responsible for her daughter's look of fatigue and strain, but this seemed reassuring rather than ominous tonight. For the first time in two months, Candace's appetite was vigorous and food tasted the way it should. So did the lime juice and mineral water she ordered.

Maddy was bouncy and happy and wanted to climb the Harbour Bridge the next day.

'Richard Gardner told me all about it,' she said. 'It takes three hours or something. It's supposed to be incredible.'

'The Harbour Bridge?' Elaine said. 'You mean the big, black one near where we bought the opals? The famous one? You can't be serious!'

'They clip you onto the rails, or a cable, or whatever. You can't possibly fall. They give you windbreakers. Grammy, don't you think it would have to be just totally, like, ba-a-d?'

'Mom…' Candace said. Elaine was looking excited, and that couldn't be good.

'Oh, let's do it, darling! The three girls? It'd be like that fad a few years ago for walking on hot coals. If I can do this, I can do anything, sort of thing.'

'But the bridge…'

'You're not afraid of heights, are you?'

No, I'm pregnant, and even if they do let pregnant women climb the bridge, I'm not sure that I'd feel safe about it…

'I'd want to hold onto the back of Maddy's collar the whole way, like I used to when she was little and liked to balance on things,' she fudged.

'Stay at the hotel, then,' Elaine offered, almost too easily, after a telling beat of silence. 'Or watch us through binoculars from the Opera House. But we're going to do it, aren't we, Maddy?'

'You're great, Grammy.'

'Darling, when it comes to the point I probably will be a teensy bit scared, so you will look after me, won't you?'

I should have known then that she'd guessed everything, Candace would say to herself later. She was playing the part of fun-loving grandmother just a little bit *too* well…

'I don't know how she can sleep with her hair over her face like that,' Elaine commented in the sitting room of their suite at six-thirty the next morning.

Coming out of her room in a pale blue silk dressing-gown, she had peeked in on Maddy, observed that she was still asleep and quietly closed the door. Candace hadn't bothered to close it behind her when she'd awoken and slipped out of the same room a few minutes ago. She hadn't intended to make any noise.

But Elaine obviously planned to talk, and didn't want to waken her granddaughter. Not just out of concern for the importance of Maddy's beauty sleep either.

'Do you want to start from the beginning, or shall I just ask questions?' she said to Candace.

'That's already a question, isn't it?'

'And shall we order room service? A hot breakfast?'

'That's two more questions!'

'You ought to eat properly. Maddy can choose what she wants later.'

'Actually, yes, I am pretty hungry.'

Starving! Eggs, bacon, sausages, grilled tomatoes, three cups of milky decaf coffee and about six pieces of wholewheat toast.

She picked up the room-service menu, then felt her mother's calculating look. She flushed.

'Is it what I think?' Elaine asked.

'That entirely depends on what it is that you think, doesn't it?'

'Well, I don't want to say it, in case I'm way off base, but...' She ticked the items off on her fingers. 'You look exhausted, you're drinking decaf coffee, you wouldn't have wine or a cocktail or even a sip of my champagne last night, and then when you said you didn't want to climb that bridge...'

Candace slumped onto the polished cotton of the couch, with the room-service menu on her lap. 'You're not way off base,' she said.

'Who's going to say it first, then?'

'You are, Mom.'

'You're pregnant, aren't you?'

'Yes.' The word was leaden.

'In the queasy stage?'

'No, yesterday I got to the starving stage.'

'Then it must have...?'

'Yes, it *did* happen pretty early on. We weren't being careless, it was just one of those things. A failure of the technology.'

'Are you still seeing him? Maddy would have said something, wouldn't she?'

'It was a sore point for her so we're taking a break. After she goes...and you. I don't know why I kidded myself that you wouldn't guess eventually, but I think you've outdone yourself in clairvoyance this time, Mom!'

'It's not clairvoyance, Candy. I just care about you so I notice what's going on.'

'After you go, I—I'm not sure what will happen.'

'You were supposed to have a wonderful vacation fling while you were here, darling, but—'

'Yes, I sussed that was your plan.'

'*Sussed?*'

Candace shrugged. 'It's a word I've picked up. It's useful. I'm planning to import it to Boston.'

'But you weren't supposed to take it this far,' Elaine accused lightly.

'It wasn't—' Candace began.

'No, of course it wasn't planned, but—'

'I was absolutely thrilled about it at first.'

'Because you were in love with him.'

'No.' Candace shook her head. Twice. 'I mean, I *am* in love with him…'

She stopped. It was the first time she'd said it aloud. And it felt so *necessary* that she said it again, listening to the words, savouring them. 'I'm in love with him, and I'm thrilled, still thrilled, about the baby. I never wanted to stop at one. That was Todd.'

Her mother cut in with an epithet concerning Todd that she would have absolutely forbidden Maddy to use.

'But—Mom—there's a problem. Might be.' She couldn't say it coherently. 'We had a test. It might have Down's.'

'Oh, Candy!'

'Which is—' She broke off. Began again. 'I mean, people manage. It would be hard—but I already love this baby. Only with the distance... Could I make my life here? Does he want me to? It'd be a whole lot more difficult for him to do it the other way around, professionally. I don't even know if he feels the way I do.'

'How could he not? My daughter? Any man with any sense—'

'Thanks, but you're my mother.' She managed a laugh. 'It doesn't count.'

'You said *might* have Down's?'

'We should find out this coming week. There was this ambiguous indicator on the scan.' She sketched the facts briefly.

'And you said "we".'

'He's not going to abandon the baby. He'll at least visit. Send presents. Want photos.'

'But you think he might abandon you? As a lover?'

'I said to him at the very beginning that I just wanted an affair.' She laughed shortly. '*Why* did I say that?'

'And to him that was a plus,' Elaine came in. 'Because he's not looking for a commitment. Only now you've changed your mind.'

'Not promising, is it?'

'Men can change their minds, too, darling,' Elaine said gently. 'Despite the prevailing mythology, it's *not* just a woman's prerogative. If he did change his and ask you to stay would you do it? Do you love him that much?'

'There's Maddy. She's not really happy with Todd and Brittany. There's you.'

'There you are! There's Maddy and there's me. I'd have her to live with me in a New York minute, if that would help.'

'She'd like that. Her father might not.'

'Her father would have to lump it, as far as I'm concerned. Would *you* like it? Leave Maddy and me out of this.'

'My career at home—'

'Leave your career out of it. Will the test result on the baby make a difference? Can you separate the future of this man's relationship with the baby from the future of his relationship with you? And, I repeat, do you love him that much?'

'I—I don't know.'

'Then you've got some thinking to do, haven't you?' came the gentle suggestion.

Candace nodded silently, then watched, still slumped on the slippery couch, while Elaine politely stole the room-service menu from her lap.

CHAPTER TEN

'Show me the beach, Maddy,' Elaine said to her granddaughter on Sunday evening, in her most imperious I'm-a-senior-citizen-so-you-have-to-do-what-I-want voice. 'Your mom's had a long drive. She needs some time by herself.'

'It's getting dark, Grammy.'

'I need some fresh air.'

'OK. I guess it won't kill me.'

'Well, the bridge climb didn't.'

'Oh, Grammy, it was so great, wasn't it? You were right, I'm gonna think back to it and know I can do *anything* now.'

'As long as you run most of those "anythings" past your mother or me first, OK?'

They headed for the door, and Candace phoned Steve as soon as they'd gone, knowing that her mother had got herself and Maddy out of the way for exactly that reason.

'Do you want to come over?' he asked at once.

'Uh, no, it's fine. Just wanted to tell you I'm planning to call Dr Strickland's office first thing tomorrow. Surely he'll have a result by then!'

'Do you want me to be there?'

'I think I do, yes.'

'You think?'

'I do. I know I do. I just don't want—'

'You're not pressuring me, OK?' he insisted. 'Are you going to ring from home or from your office, or where?'

'My office, I guess.'

'Strangely enough, I've suddenly thought of a patient I need to come and consult you about.'

'It's all right. Gillian won't ask questions, and Linda's not there on Monday mornings.'

'Sure you don't want me to come over tonight?'

'Mom and Maddy won't be gone long.'

'I'd like to meet your mother.'

'Not tonight, Steve.' Her tension had pushed to breaking point now, and she didn't want to bring the two halves of her universe together tonight, no matter how well behaved everyone was.

Steve arrived at her office the next morning only moments after she'd walked through the door herself, but it was a wasted trip. Dr

Strickland wasn't in his rooms, and his receptionist had no information on the test.

'He'll call you when he has the result,' she
promised in a voice of professional sympathy.

'Does he have my pager number?' Candace
demanded, jittery and sick. 'And the number
of the recovery annexe at the hospital?'

'I'll take those down for you,' said the same
patient voice. 'He'll phone you as soon as he
can.'

'Nothing?' Steve correctly guessed when
she'd put down the phone.

'Nothing.' She gave a thin shrug.

'What are you thinking?' he demanded.
'You're frowning.'

'I'm thinking about the intractable, un-
bridgeable chasm between doctors and patients,' she said. 'Thinking about how many
times I've left those sorts of phone calls until
the end of the day, even when I've had a result
on my desk first thing in the morning, because
I've been too flat out with other stuff, blithely
ignoring the fact that an extra eight hours of
waiting feels like eight weeks to the patient
concerned.'

'You're going to reform from now on?'

'I can't!' she answered. 'Realistically, next
time it happens I'm going to have another per-

son on hold on the phone while I'm glancing through the pathology reports, I'm going to be running late for surgery, the patient's not going to be picking up the phone if I do squeeze in a call over lunch, and it's going to get left until the end of the day.'

'Sounds like a familiar story.'

'And I know Ian Strickland has fifty other patients he's thinking about today, and some of those patients—infertility cases, people with cancer—would *wish* they were in my position, waiting for my kind of news.'

She gave a laugh that was more like a sob, and he came around the desk to where she sat and wrapped his arms around her from behind, pressing his cheek against hers.

'Don't torture yourself,' he said. 'Do you have all my numbers? Because as soon as Strickland does reach you, I want you to do your damnedest to reach me.'

'I will,' she promised.

'And we're going to see each other tonight whether we have a result or not. Maddy can have a tantrum about it if she likes.'

'She won't. Mom's very good at keeping Maddy's feet on the ground.'

'Come over for dinner, the three of you.'

'No, not that.'

She said it too quickly. Just couldn't face the thought of all those vibes. Mom trying to assess this man who'd made her daughter pregnant. Maddy feeling hostile. Steve pretending everything was fine and normal and easy.

He was silent for a moment, then said, 'She knows, doesn't she? Your mother? About the pregnancy.'

'Gee, you're almost as clairvoyant as she is!'

'What did she say?'

'A fair bit. Most of it pretty good. Gave me some things to think about.'

Another short silence, as if he wanted to ask more. But he didn't. 'I should go,' he said instead.

'I hope you'll hear from me.'

'So do I.'

Dr Strickland phoned at four o'clock. Candace had a patient with her, but had told Gillian that she wanted this particular call put through at once, no matter what.

'Yes, Dr Strickland?' She was dizzy and sick with apprehension, and drenched in clamminess.

'I have the result on your chorionic biopsy in front of me.'

'Yes?'

He didn't waste words. 'Good news, Dr Fletcher.'

'How good?'

'The best. You're carrying a healthy— Did you want to know the sex?'

'No... Yes. *Yes!*'

'It's a boy who's genetically normal in everything we're able to test for. On this occasion, that thickened skin at the nuchal fold which we noted on the scan was insignificant.'

'Th-thank you,' she stammered. '*Thank you!*' Then she gabbled to her elderly patient, Stan Caldecott, 'Will you please excuse me for a moment, Mr Caldecott?'

She fled the office, ignored Gillian's startled look, paced up and down the deserted corridor outside the rooms she shared with Linda, gave several dry, shaky sobs, then had to stand there for several moments, bringing her breathing and her expression under control.

She gave Mr Caldecott his post-surgery check-up on autopilot, deeply thankful that he was the last patient of the day, and the moment he was out the door she closed it and turned to the phone. Tried Steve's rooms. Was told he'd left for the day. Tried his mobile phone. Reached him in the middle of the supermarket.

'It's normal,' she said shakily. 'He's a boy. And he's fine. Completely fine.'

'Lord, I just want to see you!' came Steve's voice, husky and deep, different from usual yet achingly familiar.

'Yes,' she answered. 'Yes!'

'Right now.'

'Yes. I don't think I should drive. I'm—'

'I'll be there, OK? *Don't leave!*'

She didn't, although the minutes dragged until his arrival.

Gillian had obviously noticed Candace's agitation as she wandered out of her consulting room and into the rear office, ran her fingers automatically through a drawer of files and wandered out again. Darting into Candace's consulting room, the receptionist said in a stage whisper, 'Is everything all right?'

'I've just had some good news. Very good news. Family. Private.' She waved a hand. 'I'm…light-headed with relief.'

'That's great, Dr Fletcher. I'll head off, then, shall I?'

'Yes. Fine.'

Gillian left and then Steve arrived, lunged through the waiting room without the slightest pause and took her in his arms. He brushed her mouth with his lips, buried his face in the tendrils of hair that had slipped free of their clip, stroked her back and then squeezed her and lifted her from the ground to whirl her around the room.

'You're crazy!' she accused, laughing. 'Completely!'

They were both a little crazy that night. When they had calmed down enough to think, Candace phoned her mother at the beach house and told her the news.

'You can start living again now,' Elaine said.

'Yes, that's what it feels like. As if my whole life has been on hold these past three weeks. Steve's here and we're going to... Well, I don't know what we're going to do, but I might not be home for a couple of hours, OK?'

'If you get home before midnight, my girl, I'll ground you for a week!' Elaine said.

There was no danger of Candace getting home before midnight. Steve drove her up to Braidwood for dinner, and it was more than an hour's trip each way.

'I'm sorry. I hope this is all right,' he said as they looped and curved along the forested highway. 'But I need to cover some ground and feel some speed under my wheels.'

'It's fine. I think I'm the same. I'm just so happy for *him*, Steve. That he's going to come into the world now with everything going for him, instead of with such a struggle ahead.'

'I thought maybe we were going to have to step off a cliff-edge today, but we don't. It's good. We're having a boy!'

'Haven't had one of those before.' She laughed with a secret joy and delight that no words could have expressed.

'Smell this forest,' he said a moment later. 'Don't you love this? This is the lungs of the planet.'

She took a deep, appreciative breath of the air coming through the open car window, as he was doing. 'The planet's been sucking on breath mints.'

'No! Gee, Candace, is that how it smells to you? It's so much fresher than that.'

'Australians are so weird about the smell of eucalyptus!'

'And proud of it!'

She humoured the father of her child. 'It's beautiful. The sunset is beautiful, too.'

The little town of Braidwood, with its well-preserved 150-year-old buildings, was chilly but clear-skied. They weren't dressed for fine dining, so chose a quiet little place that served pizzas baked in a wood-fired oven. They were piping hot, crisp, flavourful and delicious.

They didn't linger too long over the meal. Steve bought a bottle of red wine from the hotel bottle-shop and Candace allowed herself the first small half-glass of alcohol she'd drunk since learning of her pregnancy. He had only one glass as well, and they corked up the bottle and brought it with them.

'For next time,' Steve said.

'Good wine doesn't keep for long.'

'Next time won't be long away, will it?'

They wandered around the town, window-shopped in front of a couple of antique and craft shops and indulged in a flight of total fantasy about purchasing and renovating one of the old stone public buildings, set in spacious grounds. They argued about heritage paint colours and about whether to keep the hotchpotch of outbuildings at the back or pull them down. They bought imaginary horses and landscaped a fantasy swimming pool.

They talked about politics and music and travel, enjoying the sheer pleasure of being able to bat a subject back and forth like a ping-pong ball without it all being part of some painful undercurrent of awareness, a way of *not* talking about what really filled their minds—*is the baby all right?*

They didn't have to think that way any more. The baby *was* all right. He was a boy. He was real and normal. The shadow was gone.

Then it became too cold, so they drove back to Narralee, and didn't even talk about where Steve should park the car.

At his place.

'Mom said I wasn't allowed to get home before midnight...' she said as they came up his external stairs.

'That's a challenge I can rise to without any trouble at all.'

He had his arms around her before they were even inside.

It took days for the mood of light-headed happiness to wear off, and what was left behind was something richer—a contentment, though that word didn't seem strong enough, that Candace had never felt before.

She was newly energised, light on her feet, starving hungry...and she could feel the baby now. Her unborn son. No movements yet, but a distinct, slightly rounded hardness in her lower abdomen which she knew would grow daily.

People would soon have to be told. A few weeks ago, this had seemed like a huge hurdle, but it had faded into insignificance against the question of the baby's well-being, and Candace wasn't going to get her priorities wrong any more. It didn't matter if people knew. It didn't matter what they thought.

Only Maddy's feelings mattered. This was the only reason she still hugged the secret of her pregnancy to herself. She needed to find the right time to tell Maddy.

It came on a Sunday night, halfway through Elaine's visit, when Candace had counted off the fifteen-week milestone. Not the right time, but the inevitable time.

Steve had had the three of them to lunch, along with Matt and Helen and their young children, Jake, Claire and Annabelle, and the afternoon had stretched on until Maddy had whispered to Candace, 'Mom, I'm so *bored*! I mean, the kids are cute, but—'

'You can leave if you like.' She had pressed the front-door key into her daughter's hand.

Maddy's departure—managed with accept-able politeness and grace, to Candace's re-lief—had allowed the adults to enjoy another hour of conversation, and Candace had warmed increasingly to Steve's brother and sister-in-law. When Steve touched her openly a couple of times, she knew that seeds of understanding were sprouting rapidly in Matt's and Helen's minds. Candace and Steve were both laying the groundwork. But for what?

When Candace and her mother got home from Steve's, Maddy was at first sulky, then very vocal over dinner.

'Richard and Julia phoned when I got home. They'd been trying since noon, they said, and, of course, we forgot the cellphone. I could have gone to their place, but no-o-o. Instead, the most boring afternoon of my life. Why did we have to meet those people? Why were you trying so hard to be nice to them?'

'Oh, was I?' Candace was a little startled by this.

More so when her mother confirmed it.

'They won't have noticed, darling,' Elaine reassured her. 'We only did because we know you. You were wearing your best party voice and you'd starched your laugh. Don't you think it's about time you told her?' she added, without the slightest change of tone.

If she was hoping to slip the question past Maddy, she was destined for disappointment.

'Told me what?' came the sharp demand at once. 'I know about Steve. You haven't been sneaking out to meet him. I thought you'd taken my advice and it was over.'

'Whether it's over or not,' Elaine said, 'there's going to be...'

She stopped.

Candace glared at her mother, then immediately wished she *had* let Elaine bite the bullet. Realistically, there was never going to be an easy time for it.

Maddy, I'm pregnant.

'I'm not sure what's going to happen between us in the future, Maddy,' she forced herself to say, as calmly as possible. 'We... haven't talked about that. But there's one sense in which it's never going to be over. It's the same way with your father and me, despite what happened with the divorce. When you have a child with someone, they'll always be a part of your life.'

'You mean...?' Maddy choked, flushed and looked down at Candace's stomach.

'Yes. I'm pregnant.'

'That is just—! That is just—! *How could you?* Brittany was bad enough, but at least she's *young*! God, I'm going to be so embarrassed!'

She stumbled out of the room, her eyes narrowed and burning, her cheeks flushed and her whole gangly yet graceful teenage body looking like one big scowl. The door of her room slammed.

One day she's going to have to think of a more original punctuation point to her angry exits, Candace thought. The door-slamming is getting old.

The humour was grim, and she kept it to herself.

'That went well,' she said aloud instead, the sarcasm light but deadly.

'You didn't really think it could, did you?'

'No, of course I didn't, Mom. But I thought perhaps she might be concerned about a few issues that are actually *relevant*, like distance and commitment, instead of my age and her embarrassment.'

'Now you're being as selfish as she is.'

'Oh, I am? Oh, thanks!'

'Honey—'

'Maybe I'll slam a door or two as well. Maybe we all should. Just not speak to each other for the rest of your stay.'

'We'll be going in a week,' Elaine reminded her helpfully.

'I know.' Candace paced the room. 'And I'm terrified because I don't know when I'll see you again. I don't know anything.'

'Not even what you want?'

'Not even what I want,' Candace said. 'Or what I have the right to ask. Of you, of Maddy, or of Steve.'

The atmosphere was tense and unsettled between the three of them for the remainder of Elaine's and Maddy's stay, and Candace was weighed down by mixed feelings when she drove them to Sydney for their Saturday afternoon departure. Maddy still hadn't said one pleasant word about the baby. She'd been uncomfortable enough about Brittany's pregnancy, but her feelings seemed even stronger about this one. Totally hostile. She didn't have a moment to spare for Candace's stubborn, illogical joy about the healthy boy growing inside her.

How is she going to be to live with if I go back early, when I'm sticking out like an extra shelf, and later, when my energy's consumed with a newborn? Can our relationship survive, or will there be permanent damage? Candace wondered.

Whenever she thought about Maddy's feelings, she was torn between anger and an understanding that didn't help her to find solutions.

The anger was selfish in many ways. Elaine had recognised this, and so did Candace herself. The recognition didn't always help in keeping the feeling at bay.

Nothing helped.

In four weeks, she would be halfway through her pregnancy. Three months after that, she would no longer be permitted on an international flight. If she was going to cut her stay here short and have the baby back home, that decision had to be made soon. Handling her own prenatal care, as she had been doing so far, wasn't going to be satisfactory for much longer.

She could check her own blood pressure and blood sugar, check her weight gain and her urine for the presence of protein, but she didn't have much experience of obstetrics, and didn't trust that she'd pick up on a more obscure problem, or that she'd be able to accurately assess the baby's size and growth.

At her age—'Yes, Maddy, thanks for the birthday cake you made me last week, but you're right, thirty-nine *is* old,' she told her daughter in imagination as she drove south from the airport—and after such a long gap in her child-bearing, she wanted to see someone with a lot of experience.

She would go to a top Boston obstetrician if she went home, and perhaps to Graeme Boland, down at Harpoon Bay, if she stayed here. He had a good reputation, she knew. Not down-to-earth Linda, although Linda's reputation was good as well. Linda was too close.

At the moment, however, Boston seemed the more likely place.

Why, though?

Steve was waiting for her when she reached home after the drive back from Sydney, as she had half known he would be. There was a note to that effect on her front door.

'Come straight down. I'll be home. I'll leave a message on your machine if I'm called out.'

After checking her machine and finding no message, she went, eager to see him without the stress of knowing that her mother and her daughter were close at hand.

He opened the door before she'd even knocked. His chest was bare and brown and his jeans hung precariously on his hips, as if he didn't particularly want them to stay up. She loved the way that line of hair, black against the light nutmeg brown of his skin, arrowed down the centre of his lower stomach towards his groin.

'Hello, lover,' he said, and the endearment spoke of sex, in the low, caressing tone he used.

It spoke of the passion that lay at the heart of their relationship, and she thought, Yes, I've missed it terribly, just as much as he has.

His hunger for her glittered in his blue eyes, and his impatience showed in his hands. Without another word, he lifted her jaw with the caress of his forefinger and brought his mouth down to ravish hers. Then he touched her. Everywhere, it seemed.

His hands roved across her breasts, stopping only long enough to ensure that they were swollen and ready for him before dropping to her hips to pull her closer. He slid his hands inside the back of her snug-fitting stretch pants to cup her bottom.

'I haven't seen you naked for so long.'

'Two weeks. Less.' The night they'd found out about their healthy son.

'That's long.' He peeled her cotton knit top up beneath her armpits and skimmed the balls of his thumbs across her tight nipples.

'Yes... Yes, it is.'

She clung to the waistband of his jeans with two sets of curled fingers, like hanging onto the safety rail on a carnival ride. Her knuckles pressed into the warm, tanned skin at his waist, and she flung her head back and closed her eyes, gasping in delight at the continuing onslaught of his hands and his mouth.

'Let me undress you,' he said, sliding her pants down over her hips. 'Let me see you...'

'And you,' she said huskily. 'Not fair if you get all the pleasure.'

They didn't talk properly until afterwards. A long time afterwards. Not until they'd eaten the meal he'd prepared for her and curled up together on the couch with music playing in the background.

'Maddy and your mother got off all right, did they?'

'Yes, fine. I stopped on the way back at that spot where we picnicked, under the Norfolk pines, and watched their plane take off.'

'Silly!'

'Why?'

'I bet you cried.'

'Was that wrong?'

'No, I guess it wasn't,' he answered. 'Of course it wasn't. Just seems like you set yourself up for it, going to that spot where the planes look so dramatic and the sense of distance is so huge.'

'The distance *is* huge.'

An awareness hung in the air. Not of sex, for once, but the awareness of unspoken things. Problems. Decisions.

Candace was swamped with a painful need to have Steve take control of this, of their future.

Ask me to stay. *Please!* No, *tell* me to stay. Fight for me if you want me. Tell me we can work it out with Maddy and everyone else. Tell me nothing else matters but the fact that we love each other. Tell me that love can always find a way.

It was all clamouring so loudly inside her head that she was convinced he must hear it. Couldn't he feel the way her muscles had knotted? Her whole body was pressed against his side, length to length. He must be able to feel it.

But he said nothing. Until finally words came. 'Are you staying tonight?'

His voice sounded creaky, rusty, as if he'd been half-asleep, or something.

'I don't think I will.'

Maybe if she hadn't dressed again earlier. She had thought of just slipping into one of his

T-shirts as she'd done once or twice before. There was something so intimate about that, surrounding herself in the cleanness and subtlety of his scent, swimming inside the garment because he was bigger than she was, casually claiming the right to borrow his clothes.

But she hadn't done it tonight. Instead, she was fully dressed, and it was easy to go.

Better to go. She probably needed some time alone anyway—some time to think about the stark fact that, with all that they'd been through, he hadn't said that he loved her.

'Sure?' he queried. 'I'd like you to.'

I'd love you to? I love you? Sorry, no, it didn't even come close! If he felt it, he needed to say it. And if he didn't feel it…

Out of self-preservation, she hardened her heart.

'Best not.'

She eased herself out of his arms and walked towards the door, turning halfway there to face him. 'I need some time to myself, Steve. I've had Maddy for four and a half weeks, and Mom for two. Now I just need to think.'

'Want to think here? Out loud?'

As an offer, it still wasn't nearly good enough. She shook her head.

'OK, then,' he said.

He kept watching her, and she couldn't tear her gaze away.

'Busy tomorrow?' So casual. Surely he cared more than that!

'I'm not sure,' she answered.

'All right, Candace.' He got up, looking restless now. 'Maybe I'll drop over to your place.'

'I'll…' She hesitated. How much of a stand did she want to take? 'I'll leave you a note if I'm going out.'

'Do that,' Steve said.

Then he watched as she let herself out, standing frozen in the middle of his living room. He didn't move from the spot until quite a long while after she'd gone, and even when he did, it was only to pace restlessly out to his deck to let the air clear out his aching head.

He felt like howling at the moon. Instead, he just gave a shuddering groan.

When he'd asked if she was staying, he'd been so painfully tempted to leave off the last word, 'tonight'. So tempted to make it into a bigger question. *The* big question. The one he sensed she was grappling with as well. They were having a baby together, but they lived on opposite sides of the world. He couldn't just ask her to 'stay' as if it was easy.

If this was just about now, he could have said it in a heartbeat. Stay tonight. Stay for a week. Stay as long as you want.

But it wasn't about now, not even a stretchy, open-ended now. It was about forever. Was he arrogant enough to ask her to stay? Was he humble enough to follow her? Forever?

'Stay forever.' He tried the words on his tongue, speaking them quietly into the chilly night, and they frightened him. He tried them again, with a difference. 'I need you. Stay forever.'

It still didn't work. It wasn't fair. If he was going to say, 'Stay forever,' then he had to be damned sure about what he was promising, about the value of what he had to give. He had to be very arrogant indeed, in the face of what he'd be asking her to sacrifice, and he didn't know how to find that certainty and that arrogance to set against the doubts he sensed in her, and the complexities in her life.

'I'll follow you.' That wasn't any easier. Maddy was at a difficult age. Would Candace want her daughter to have a stepfather hanging around, not really quite old enough for the job?

Speaking of hanging around, would one of them stay at home with the baby, or would they both work? Candace's position as an attending surgeon would be considerably senior to anything he could get in the United States for the first few years. It was demanding, too. Not the sort of thing she could tackle part time. He might end up as the one at home. A certain humility on his part would definitely be a requirement. He wasn't a particularly humble person.

They hadn't talked about any of this at all, and he had no idea about what she would want. No idea. It was a problem. He was waiting for her to come up with some answers, trying to be fair to her, and it wasn't working.

Nothing in their relationship was working at all. Damn, he had to take control of this, take the courage and the arrogance to push both of them blindly forward without knowing where it might end.

A fire of rebellion began to build inside him, flaring with incredible speed. What time was it? Ten? Later? He didn't care. He wasn't going to leave this any longer. He'd been wrong to let her go home alone tonight. She didn't have the right to weigh her options and make her decisions alone. They had to do it together.

CHAPTER ELEVEN

INSIDE the house, Steve grabbed a light jacket off a hook on the back of the door, checked his pocket and belt for keys and pager and loped out the door, almost at a run.

He was halfway down the stairs when he felt the buzz of the pager against his hip. It wasn't the first time it had interrupted him when he'd had Candace on his mind...or lying against his heart as they'd made love. They'd had the usual couldn't-have-come-at-a-worse-moment intrusions because of his profession. 'Phonus interruptus' another GP in his practice called it.

This one, he thought, had to take first prize for bad timing.

He checked the code on the readout, and it was the most obvious one—the one that meant, 'Your presence at the hospital is required. Accident and Emergency Department, please.'

He climbed into the car and got there in seven minutes, ready to be peeved—or maybe to explode—if he wasn't really needed. With

Candace. That was where he wanted to be. Not here.

He was needed, though. Coming into the emergency department through a side door, he found the place brightly lit. Night Sister Jenny Shearer was pleased to see him so promptly. Behind her, he glimpsed one of the cubicles set up with equipment and a figure making a mound on the bed.

He didn't know this patient, Christine Smith. She wasn't local. Down from chilly Canberra for a winter break in the warmer climate of the coast. She had her husband Neil and two-year-old son Liam with her. She was twenty-nine weeks pregnant and her membrane had torn, leaking a persistent trickle of straw-yellow amniotic fluid and stimulating painful but intermittent contractions.

They could have dealt with the situation here if it had just been a matter of having her on bed-rest. There wasn't a lot that could be or needed to be done. Strict bed-rest, good fluid intake, monitoring of the contractions, checking for signs of infection.

The problem came with the fact that with a leaking amniotic sac, Christine had a ninety per cent chance of going into unstoppable labour over the next forty-eight hours. They didn't have high-level neonatal care facilities here. If the baby was born here, he or she wouldn't survive.

Steve wasn't at all surprised that Sister Shearer had already arranged for a SouthCare helicopter to make a night flight from Canberra to pick up the patient and transport her to Black Mountain Hospital. There the baby would have a fighting chance, at twenty-nine weeks, of surviving a premature birth with no long-term problems. Since the flight was short, Mrs Smith was unlikely to deliver during the journey.

On paper, Steve's job was to keep the patient stable until the SouthCare team arrived, then assist with the transfer. In reality, it was much more about reassurance, listening and answering questions.

'What happens if I get an infection? What are my chances of going to my due date?'

'Can I come with her in the helicopter? If this settles, will she be allowed home? I'm not sure if I can take the time off work...'

Steve fielded all this as best he could. They seemed like a nice family—young and steady, the parents trying to conceal their anxiety from their little boy, whom they'd had to waken from sleep at their motel, and who now looked frazzled and disorientated.

'Mummy,' he was saying persistently. 'Mummy...'

It turned into open crying, and Christine asked, 'Could he come up here on the bed, or something? Neil, should you just take him back to the motel straight away? It's insane for you to wait till I go, and then drive up to Canberra tonight.'

They talked about it, then Christine's face crumpled as another contraction came. 'They're only light,' she said. Saying it so it would come true, Steve understood. 'Seems like they might stop.'

Steve heard Neil mutter through pale, dry lips, 'This isn't fun. I hate this!'

But then the air began to shudder with the sound of the helicopter approaching outside, and everything got hectic. Liam had fallen asleep on his father's shoulder. Christine was coming out with all sorts of distracted last-minute instructions to her husband about her little son's care. His breakfast. His tantrums. Travis the toy tractor.

Steve watched the helicopter take off and was about to leave the hospital himself when he noticed a familiar car pulling up in one of the parking spaces to the side of the emergency entrance. His brother Matt's car.

His heart lurched, but Matt had seen him and was rolling his eyes when he got out of the car.

'Don't panic. It's OK,' he said. 'Annabelle has got a peanut up her nose. Put it there herself, of course, and didn't tell us because she was scared we'd be cross. We only found out about it when she woke up and was crying in bed because it hurt.'

He bundled his three-and-a-half-year-old daughter out of her booster seat and carried her into the A and E department. Wearing a pink dressing-gown on top of flannel pyjamas, she was looking big-eyed and ready to cry.

'Hey, didn't I tell you we might see Uncle Steve here?' Matt told his daughter in a bright tone. 'He's going to get that peanut out, and if you're a big brave girl about it, I bet he'll have a...'

'Jelly bean and a sticker,' Steve supplied.

'Hear that, Annabelle? A jelly bean and a sticker for you.' In an aside to Steve, he added, 'Fun, this is!'

'Do you get much of this sort of fun in the parenthood game?' Steve asked casually, although he knew what the answer would be.

'It's a laugh a minute,' Matt drawled, then took a second look at Steve's face. 'You're not thinking of—?'

'I'm working a few things out,' Steve cut in hastily. His scalp was tight and he was now even more desperate to get away. To get to Candace. To explode at her about rights and decisions and the future. Hell, she'd be asleep by now, probably, but he was too impatient and angry to wait. Too desperately in love with her as well. 'Let's look at that peanut, Annabelle,' he said, his voice a gritty rasp, overlaid with effortful good cheer.

Annabelle was a very big, brave girl, mainly because the peanut wasn't lodged all that far up her nose. Matt or Helen could have got it out themselves, only she'd kicked and screamed when they'd tried, and they'd become concerned about accidentally shoving it further in.

Uncle Steve in his doctor clothes was apparently intimidating enough to induce co-operation. Or perhaps it was the prospect of the sticker and the jelly bean. Matt and Annabelle were ready to leave again in a few minutes, as soon as they'd made a trip to the bathroom.

'What I said before about fun...' Matt said urgently outside the bathroom door, when he saw that Steve was about to head off.

'I know,' he reassured his elder brother. 'Don't worry. You haven't put me off. I know it can't always be fun.'

Over the past few weeks, without him being fully aware of how his attitude was changing, the job description had come to make sense.

'When you're with the right person, you can take whatever comes,' Matt said. 'Helen and I have found that out this year, if we didn't know it before. Don't let Candace get away just because there are a few hurdles, mate. You can get over those.'

He pressed a fist against Steve's upper arm.

'I know,' Steve repeated. 'I know, OK? Let me get on with it, Matt.'

'Now?'

'Now!' he confirmed grimly. 'Should have been weeks ago.'

Although she had craved solitude when she left Steve's, her own house seemed too empty when Candace closed the front door behind her. Elaine's bag no longer hung over the back of a chair. Maddy's magazines had been piled away, and her litter of hair accessories was gone from the bathroom.

Candace wandered through the living room and down to the bedrooms. Maddy and Elaine hadn't vanished without trace, she was reminded when she breasted their doorway. Their twin beds were covered with the many fruits of their shopping expeditions.

There were at least twenty items which Elaine had casually asked Candace to 'mail back for us'. Elaine had gone so far as to acquire boxes, bubble wrap and packing tape, but she hadn't actually done any of the packing.

Candace picked up a heavy kitchen cutting board made of Australian hardwoods, measured out a section of bubble wrap and parcelled up the smooth rectangle of wood. It fitted very neatly into the bottom of one of the boxes, but maybe an extra layer of bubble wrap wouldn't go amiss...

Before she knew it, she was fully engrossed in the job, and decided that she may as well keep going until she'd finished. It wasn't as if she was going to get to sleep yet, and she could think just as well while her hands were busy. Better, maybe. For good measure, she put on some soft music and made coffee as well.

Thinking. Decisions.

Have the baby here, or go back to Boston? Taking Steve out of the picture, only one thing made sense. To go home. The idea beckoned, yet at the same time seemed to suggest bitter failure.

I won't decide yet. I'll leave it a little longer.

No, that was weak. She couldn't afford, emotionally, to keep herself on hold for Steve any longer. If he cared the way she did, surely he'd have said something by now? Her thoughts circled back to the beginning, dwelt on Maddy and Mom, Todd and Brittany and their baby, returned once more to Steve.

It was after midnight when she heard footsteps pounding up her stairs. It frightened her until she recognised their familiar rhythm. Going to the door with some tape and a half-wrapped souvenir mug still in her hands, she knew it would be Steve. Didn't know whether to be angry or grateful.

He was turning up at this time of night? Hadn't she told him she needed to be alone? Hadn't her spirit cried out for him to give her some help? The two sets of feelings warred inside her like hostile siblings.

She opened the door and he strode straight inside, pivoted on one foot and began forcefully, 'I've been thinking about it, Candace, and you have no right—!' Then he stopped abruptly and his face went white. 'You're packing.'

'Y-yes, for my—'

But he didn't give her a chance to finish. Didn't notice, or maybe didn't care, how he'd unnerved her.

'No!' The word grated between his clenched teeth.

He grabbed tape, mug and bubble wrap from her hands and flung them onto the couch. He looked magnificent, hardened by anger, arrogantly certain of himself. Wounded, though, as well. He was like a jungle cat, both enraged and endowed with exaggerated strength because of his pain.

'Don't!' he said. 'You have no right— You can't just leave without some input from me. You can't leave at all.'

His grip closed around both her upper arms, and this close she was frightened at how white he looked. His eyes were like blue flame, blinding her into incoherence.

'Steve, I'm—'

'You can't leave,' he repeated for the third time.

'I'm not,' she gasped at last. 'I'm just packing this up for Mom and Maddy. The things they bought. They couldn't fit them in their suitcases, and I'm going to mail them instead.'

'Uh...!' The breath went out of him as if he'd been struck with a blow. 'That's...a help, I guess,' he said. He was still gripping her arms. 'But, no,' he went on, 'it doesn't change anything. My God, Candace, we're so far overdue for a talk it's not funny! You have no right to make any of your decisions alone!' His voice softened suddenly. 'But, of course, it's at least half my fault that you don't know that.'

His arms slid around her and she was astonished to find them trembling. So was his jaw. Trembling with tension, his whole body.

'I love you,' he said. 'God, why haven't I said it before?'

His kiss was passionate, imperious, sure of its response.

'I love you, too,' she answered, tears burning in her eyes. 'I've loved you for—I don't know when it started. Is it enough? I've been wondering if it's enough.'

'Hell, yes! *Enough?* It's the *only* thing, Candace. Maybe I didn't know it until tonight, but I know it now, and a moment ago when I thought you were packing to leave without even a word of advance warning... Loving each other is the *only* thing. We have to say it to each other—'

'We just did.'

'We have to say it every time we're together, and then we have to talk about the future, knowing that what we decide has to be based on that. The fact that we love each other. Candace, I love you, and I want to be with you, whatever it takes.'

His arms and his lips softened, as his voice had softened, and when he kissed her this time it was sweet and slow and cajoling.

'So do I,' she said, with her cheek pillowed against his chest.

'Whatever it takes?'

'I want to be with you. I want to make a family for this little boy.'

'Here? Do you want it to be here? That's one of the things that seemed like a mountain between us.'

'Anywhere.'

'Anywhere. That's almost as big as "forever"—do you realise that?' he said.

'Are you asking me about forever?' She lifted her head, cupped his face in the palms of her hands and looked deeply into it.

'I don't think I'm asking. I'm telling you,' he said, meeting her gaze steadily. 'Or I'm offering it. Forever. If you want it, Candace. I want to marry you and promise you that it's forever. As for where, it can be wherever you want. Wherever we decide. Only let's decide it together. Let's not second-guess what we think the other person needs.'

'Can it be here?'

'What about Maddy?'

'I've been thinking about that tonight. Really thinking about it, instead of running away from it because it's too confusing and scary. Maddy...' she took a deep breath '...will find it easier this way. To live with Mom, who's so good with her. That's kind of hard for me, because she's growing up and I haven't accepted it yet.'

'Mothers don't, do they?' He smiled.

She nodded. 'It's the same as it was when I first came out here. It was harder for me to leave Maddy and accept that she'd be all right than it was for her to wave goodbye to me. She's going to be sixteen soon. She'll live with Mom for a couple of years and they'll have fewer fights than Maddy and I would have, even without this baby on the scene. Mom will talk to her about the baby, and about you and me, and she'll listen and take it to heart in a way she never would if I said it. She'll make more visits over here, and we'll visit there. We'll talk on the phone and run up huge bills, and stay closer that way, I think, than if she had to live with us.'

'Yeah?'

'Two lovers, their baby and a teen? Doesn't work! That's really why she's been miserable with Todd and Brittany.' For the first time, she spoke those two names together without pain. 'It's not because she was missing me. It's not even because Todd and Brittany are particularly horrible.' Again, she could say it and it didn't hurt.

But he told her seriously, 'Candee, I'm sure they're very, very horrible.'

She laughed. 'Thanks! But when she's older and settled somewhere, could we move close by so that she can get to be friends with her second little brother?'

'I like the idea of that,' he said. 'Living there, when it seems right. I like the idea of not making it an either-or thing. We can do both. There'll be sacrifices. But when I think about what I feel, I can believe they'll be worth it, and they'll balance out.'

'The Pacific seemed so huge to me today when I watched their plane taking off,' Candace said. 'But, yes, when there's solid ground beneath my feet, the solid ground of loving you, and knowing that you feel the same, the distance doesn't seem so important.'

'Nothing else is important, everything else finds its right place, when we're so certain of this,' he whispered, and found her mouth.

EPILOGUE

THIS isn't fun, Steve thought to himself. This most definitely and absolutely isn't fun.

Candace squeezed his hand again. Lacerated it, if he was truthful. Her face was red and straining and sheened with sweat. Her blue hospital gown was limp, and she was very, very tired. Sixteen hours of labour, a quarter past four in the morning, and it wasn't over yet. He hated her pain, and his powerlessness. Hated it. Oh, truly, there were moments in this adventure called love that were definitely not fun!

But at least Candace's pain had been replaced to an extent by hard work over the past half-hour. The baby's head was crowning strongly, and no longer slipping back up into the birth canal between contractions. It wouldn't be long now.

'You're doing so great, Mom!' Maddy said with a sob in her voice. She squeezed Candace's shoulder from her position on the other side of the bed. 'I'm so proud of you.'

But Candace was too involved in her work to respond to her daughter with more than a big-eyed, love-filled, exhausted look, as another contraction came.

She and Steve had both been thrilled and relieved when Maddy had announced over the phone, several months ago, that she wanted to be present for both the wedding and the birth, if possible.

'I've talked about it a lot with Grammy, and I want to apologise for being a spoiled brat, before, when I was with you.'

'Oh, sweetheart...'

It had ended up a very lengthy phone call, and both Candace and Steve had been very happy to accommodate what Maddy wanted. The logistics of distance dictated that both events would have to take place during the same trip, over Maddy's Christmas and New Year break from school.

This had given all of them some anxious moments on 23 December when an hour of false labour made it seem as if the baby might arrive before their scheduled Christmas Eve wedding.

'Really, baby!' Elaine had admonished Candace's round, hard belly. 'It would be a lot more convenient if you would wait. Your big sister might want to see you born—personally, I'll be waiting somewhere civilised, not in the delivery suite—but I'm here to see your parents married first!'

And the labour had subsided, the simple wedding had taken place, outdoors, at seven o'clock in the evening at a local park— Candace had looked huge and fabulous in a simply cut cream linen maternity dress—and now the baby was coming, right on his due date of 7 January. As promised, Elaine was waiting for the news at home in Candace's and Steve's spare room, while Maddy was here, tired but very involved.

'Pant through the break, Candace,' coached the midwife urgently. 'His head is almost out. One more push...'

'One more push, Candee,' Steve echoed. 'You can do it.'

She nodded and gripped her angled thighs, and he held her shoulders and prayed.

'He's coming... He's coming...' the midwife said.

Candace gave a huge sound of effort, half groan, half yell. The head was out...it was rotating...the midwife delivered one shoulder...the other slipped out on its own, followed by torso and limbs, all wet and slippery.

Born! He was safely born! Steve's eyes stung then filled, and his diaphragm jerked with sobs of relief that he barely noticed. He was grinning so much that it hurt, was in no doubt at all that this was the best moment of his life.

The baby cried at once, lustily, and waved his tiny, splayed fingers. Pink spread all over his body, and the midwife cradled him in a towel and laid him at once in Candace's arms.

'Oh... Oh...' Candace said. She was crying, too. 'He's so beautiful! He's amazing! So perfect!'

Maddy had dissolved completely. 'I knew it would be special, but I didn't know it would be like this,' she said. 'Oh, Mom...'

They hugged, clumsy in their emotion, and Maddy touched her little brother's head.

'I'm so glad you were here, sweetheart,' Candace whispered to her daughter. Then she turned to Steve, frowning. Strands of hair clung damply to her forehead, making him itch to smooth them back. 'Is your hand OK? I think I was pulling on it a bit...'

'It's fine.' He hid it from sight, didn't want her to see the stiffness in it or the scratches. 'Everything's fine.'

He leaned across, pushed the hair from her brow and kissed her, then watched as she lifted her gown and gave the baby her breast. He felt a fullness inside him, a physical sensation of love and protectiveness, pride and triumph, which was almost a kind of pain.

'You know, I actually think this was all worth it,' Maddy said. She was laughing now, while brushing tears from her young face with the back of her hand. 'All the horribleness. Everything. Never thought I'd be able to say that. But it really was.'

'Is she right, Steve?' Candace whispered, looking at him across the damp black shape of their baby's head, pillowed at her breast.

'Do you even need to ask?' he whispered back.

MEDICAL ROMANCE™

Large Print

Titles for the next three months...

October

A WOMAN WORTH WAITING FOR   Meredith Webber
A NURSE'S COURAGE   Jessica Matthews
THE GREEK SURGEON   Margaret Barker
DOCTOR IN NEED   Margaret O'Neill

November

THE DOCTORS' BABY   Marion Lennox
LIFE SUPPORT   Jennifer Taylor
RIVALS IN PRACTICE   Alison Roberts
EMERGENCY RESCUE   Abigail Gordon

December

A VERY SINGLE WOMAN   Caroline Anderson
THE STRANGER'S SECRET   Maggie Kingsley
HER PARTNER'S PASSION   Carol Wood
THE OUTBACK MATCH   Lucy Clark

MILLS & BOON®

0902 LP 1P Medical